the tour guide

Based on a true story.

by Harrison Rose Tate

the tour guide

Based on a true story.

This is a work of creative nonfiction. Names, identifying details, and select events have been changed for privacy and narrative cohesion.

Published by ECS, Fallbrook, California

Cover design and interior layout by
Harrison Rose Tate

ISBN: 979-8-9987737-3-0
Library of Congress Number (LCCN): 2025917729

First Edition

For permissions or inquiries, please contact:

www.harrisonrosetate.com

author's note

In these pages, the reader will bear witness to inheritances of many kinds. I'd like to share one of my own.

As noted, this novel is based on a true story. Here's a second one. Mine.
The story behind the story.

I sat alone at an outdoor café table in San Miguel de Allende. It was an exceptionally quiet day, and I had isolated myself even further by ducking into a shaded corner at the back of Fábrica La Aurora, which is the art district in this colonial city. I was the only customer, sipping on a mineral water on a hot afternoon. It was just me and the young woman working behind the counter where I'd bought my drink. You could hear leaves rustling. Not much more.

In the distance, a small group of six or eight middle-aged people moved through the empty galleries. Most were couples. They looked American, like me. They studied the large works of art on even larger white walls. Tourists.

I had been in San Miguel for around three weeks at this point, there on an extended stay to study the language. I had finished my work for the day. I was there, momentarily, before returning to my apartment.

I've dedicated my entire career to writing, but most of my work doesn't bear my name. Corporate blogs, technical articles… the anonymous architecture of nonfiction for profit. I was comfortable, didn't need more.

A man approached the counter and ordered a beer.

He looked Latino, younger than me, and strikingly handsome. He spoke Spanish to the cashier. He chose the table next to mine, the only other seat in the shade.

He introduced himself as Santiago.

The tour guide.

Before that afternoon, I didn't have a story to tell.
I also had no knowledge of the tragic events that occurred in Peru, in 1970.

I left the café with both.

contents

THE
TOUR GUIDE

CONVENTO DE LA DIVINA MISERICORDIA
YUNGAY, PERU
1964

BASED ON A TRUE STORY

CHAPTER ONE

hymns

"Chap chap chap," said Sister Pilar as a damp cloth twisted in the nun's hands, dripping quietly into the bowl as she prepared to clean the delicate face before her.

She spoke in time with the falling of the water drops, hoping the rhythmic nature of the two sounds would calm her charge. Ana Lucia was nonverbal, yet she had managed, years ago, to immediately recognize every hymn the nuns knew. When she grew bored with them, she didn't hesitate to make that known. Loud moans echoed off the walls of the small cinder block room.

Sister Pilar knew well, in order to maintain a spiritually centered environment, secular music should be avoided. She never minded singing hymns, no matter how many times she had repeated them. Pilar had an exceptional singing voice; natural and effortless. But the talent with which she had been born was of no importance to Ana Lucia, who moaned and vocalized unintelligible syllables even louder.

She finally gave up.

"Ah, compañera," she sighed, "how about this one?"

"a Pampa y la Puna, qué lugar tan especial,

Donde el viento trae susurros y las llamas van a bailar."

Pilar sang with perfect pitch and added stylistic flourishes to the simple song. Ana Lucia was evidently pleased. She was finally peaceful and still. Her eyes slowly closed.

"El zorro se ríe del cóndor que no sabe aterrizar,

En la Pampa y la Puna, todo puede pasar."

She had already finished washing her for the day, so she ended on that note. Ana Lucia's hazel eyes fluttered open when she realized the room had gone quiet. Pilar closed the door as softly as she could, but Ana Lucia let out loud, painful groans.

There was nothing that could be done. Lately, leaving her this way was the worst part of Sister Pilar's day.

Ana Lucia was pregnant again, and her discomfort was clear.

Pilar had only recently begun caring for her.

Their beloved Mother Superior had recently retired from active ministry. She was in her late eighties and in poor health. Sub-Prioress Constanza José had been asked to take her place. When they were still both sisters in fellowship Constanza and Pilar had developed a deep and trusting bond.

During Ana Lucia's first two tragic rapes, both of which had resulted in pregnancies that horrified the convent, Sister Hermelinda had been her caretaker.

As a result, the convent and grounds were placed on lockdown day and night. The nuns took every precaution, implementing strict security measures to prevent any further violations.

But Ana Lucia became pregnant a third time anyway.

It was one of the most difficult days that Constanza, the newly appointed Mother Superior, would face in her years at the convent. She knew what she needed to do. At mealtime, she watched Hermelinda as the elder sister ate her lentils and boiled potatoes. She studied her while in prayer, where Hermelinda nodded off and struggled to stand from the kneeler. She was frail.

Sister Pilar was asked to take over Ana Lucia's care. Pilar was relentlessly reliable. Both nuns braced for Hermelinda's reaction to the reassignment.

The conversation didn't go well. Hermelinda responded to the news with visible agony. In the weeks that followed, she began to spiral. Shortly afterward, she died in her sleep of natural causes at the age of seventy-nine.

There had been two babies, both healthy, in fact, beautiful. The first was a boy, and the second, a girl. Both times, Sister Hermelinda had been greeted the next day, in the early morning hours, while it was still pitch dark. A large man on a black bicycle with dented fenders arrived each time, twenty-two months apart. The bike had a basket, first lined in dried coriander, then with small remnants of carpet and felt, and finally with a traditional woven Peruvian blanket. Although not ideal, it was soft, and safe enough. The baby would be placed carefully in the basket, and the man on the bicycle would ride off into the pre-dawn mist.

Each time, some weeks later, at the hacienda of the second wealthiest landowner in the region, Don Fernando Javier Alarcón, a new addition was welcomed into the family.

It didn't take Sister Pilar long to realize that the Don and his wife, Doña García, were infertile. The couple would hide the newborn for a short while to avoid suspicion, then joyfully announce the birth of 'their' child.

The two siblings shared a father and a biological mother, but were raised by Doña García as her own.

In a way that made her uncomfortable, Sister Pilar almost understood. Don Fernando had been open about their struggle to have children. He seemed desperate to please his wife.

Two beautiful, healthy babies born to Ana Lucia, hidden by the convent, taken, and hidden again before they were introduced to the community as the biological children of a wealthy couple. They shared their DNA with only one.

At least they would be brought up well.

When Fernando was a boy, the Alarcón family had owned quadruple the land. It was rural, but they made good use of it by farming and raising livestock. At the time, the Alarcóns were one of the rare upper-middle-class families in a region of mostly poor ones.

Fernando had a little sister he had been very attached to. She passed away at the age of seven, due to a severe bacterial infection. Fernando spent the remainder of his growing years as an only child. He buried himself in his work around the ranch to escape from his grief and loneliness. His father's friends and associates would see Fernando outside day and night, working on something or another, whenever they visited the ranch. He was not tall, but the work made him muscular. When young Fernando was not working, he was meticulous about his appearance. Mustache neatly trimmed, clothing spotless and ironed.

When he reached young adulthood, Don Fernando Senior sent his son to Lima, to the Universidad Nacional Agraria La Molina. At the time, in Yungay, it was unheard of for one to pursue higher education. Even in the capital, only the wealthiest or most ambitious families could afford to send their children to college. Fernando studied agriculture and business there. His grades were very good.

It was at the university in Lima that Fernando met his future wife, Magdalena Victoria Morales García. She was born and raised among the capital's elite, sophisticated beyond her youthful age. Thin and gazelle-like, she wore her sleek, black hair pulled back and had large, sparkling brown, doe-like eyes.

A city girl and a country boy. Despite their differences, Fernando charmed and impressed her with his intelligence and strong work ethic. Many of the young men she had grown up with in upper-class Lima were partiers, dependent on their parents' wealth. They were weak-minded, and weak-bodied due to a life of pampering.

The two were friendly for a while. After graduation, Fernando returned to Yungay.

His father was not the man he had been when his son had left. He had grown older and much more frail. It had taken nearly all the strength he had left to maintain the ranch while he waited until his son had earned his degree. Obediently, Fernando took over immediately. He wasn't prepared. He had believed he had more time. Occupied day and night, he and Magdalena drifted apart.

By the time Fernando returned, his hometown had grown exponentially and now bordered the ranch on all sides. His father passed quickly. His mother lasted a bit longer, then died peacefully in her sleep, ten months later. Fernando was left with no living relatives. The closest thing he had to family were the few servants who had worked on the ranch since he was a boy.

After his parents passed, he inherited the land. Much of the space was unneeded. Fernando made deal after deal to sell off the valuable parcels, charging a premium for each. Entire neighborhoods were developed on the properties around him. What remained of the Alarcón ranch was still so large that you could not see the new developments from his own hacienda, situated on the hilltop highest on the property.

It was then that Fernando became the second most wealthy man in all of Yungay. He used a small portion of the funds to renovate the hacienda and surrounding grounds. He imported furniture, added beautiful curtains to the large windows, modernized the kitchen and bathrooms and hung crystal chandeliers in several of the rooms. Although he was still a bachelor, he gutted a small room adjacent to the master suite, and renovated it into a dressing room to be used by a lady of the house. He knew exactly who he would like the lady of the house to be.

When it was finished, the hacienda was comparable to the finest ranches of its caliber in all of Peru. In his own mind, Fernando would only compare it to those in Lima. Would it be considered elegant by Magdalena? His newfound wealth may have been the biggest single factor to give him courage to reach back out to his college crush. Since returning to Yungay, he had thought of Magdalena daily, although he wasn't sure she would remember him.

Yet, remember him, she did. Magdalena fondly recalled how different Fernando seemed.

Arranging a visit was difficult. Magdalena's father would not allow her to travel alone. Fernando made the long journey to Lima to accompany her back to Yungay for a visit. Her father was a stern man, a businessman. He told Fernando ominously that he was lucky he was allowing his daughter to go at all. He trusted his daughter, who had promised her father they would be staying in separate rooms, although she had no idea what the arrangement would be.

Fernando returned with Magdalena to the ranch, glancing at her nervously, trying to guess her reaction.

Magdalena adored the now-elegant hacienda. The two began their courtship, visiting one another as often as they could. Eight months later, they were engaged. Eighteen months later, Magdalena's parents hosted an extravagant wedding in Lima, complete with formal Mass, live music, and a reception held in a grand colonial-era villa adorned with white linen, silver candelabras, and towering arrangements of lilies and bougainvillea. Guests sipped pisco sours under strings of lights as the newlyweds danced their first *vals criollo*. Magdalena smiled dreamily, eyes half closed, beneath a sky warm with sea air and celebration. Fernando looked down at her as they danced, captivated.

She returned to the ranch as the new lady of the house, Doña García.

As the new Doña settled in Yungay, she quickly made many friends. At times, it was a difficult adjustment to be so far from family, but she didn't mind. She and Fernando planned on starting a family.

But months passed, then a year. Doña García was still not pregnant. Fernando watched helplessly as sadness and frustration began to consume his wife. Gradually, her once-playful nature began to change. Everyone seemed to notice that the Doña was in an unrelenting state of despair.

One morning, two-and-a-half years after their wedding, Fernando was reading the newspaper in the sitting room when he noticed his wife appear quietly in the doorway. He knew exactly what was coming. She perched on the armrest of the sofa across from him and told him she wanted to leave.

Fernando was not about to let her go. It was during that conversation that he assured her he would find her a baby to "adopt". Appeased for the moment, Doña García was convinced to wait the forty weeks it would take for a baby to come. Along the way, Fernando would reassure her that things were progressing well, and it wouldn't be long before she was a mother.

When the couple was blessed not just once, but then a second time, with newborns almost immediately after Ana Lucia gave birth, nobody in the town seemed to notice any connection between the two, seemingly unrelated, incidents.

Poor Ana Lucia was so insignificant. Few even knew of her two births. The nuns certainly did not speak of them, due to the tragic nature of her assaults, and the mysterious disappearances of the babies.

One thing, however, was evident. Doña García was a wonderful mother. Word at the private Catholic academy where both children attended was that the two were bright and creative. Neither child showed signs of their biological mother's disability. The oldest, a boy, was friendly and popular. His younger sister, a bit more reserved.

Sister Pilar knew all of the nuns at the school. Word got around. Whenever the children were mentioned, she only listened intently, but never spoke of it to anyone.

CHAPTER TWO

unnamed

Take captive every thought to make it obedient to Christ, Sister Pilar recited silently from Corinthians as she walked along the slippery cobblestone street in the dewy morning. Her thoughts were again intruded upon by the mystery of Ana Lucia's third pregnancy.

Nobody outside the religious order had a key. She knew that for certain.

Ana Lucia was due any day.

She continued walking to the local outdoor market.

As Pilar placed onion, nopal, and tomatillo in her basket, a young girl, maybe eight or nine, sprinted up to her, completely out of breath. The girl looked disheveled. She interrupted the conversation between the produce seller and the nun, desperately tugging at her habit to get her attention.

She had been playing with friends after school near the convent a few minutes before.

"Novitate Ysla has sent me, dear Madre," the girl panted, "the baby of Ana Lucia is coming!"

The message had been sent by Isabel Cristina Ysla, a young woman who had recently entered the convent and had not yet taken her vows. With Sister Pilar absent at this critical moment, Isabel Cristina was overwhelmed. She was just a teenager herself. A sheltered one at that, who had grown up with an overprotective father and two brothers. Naïve and easily frightened, she was completely unprepared to handle a situation like this. She had managed to keep a clear head only long enough to summon the midwife, who had been on call for a few days now, and to send the young girl to get Sister Pilar.

Pilar practically ran back to assist with the birth, clutching her habit with one hand so that she would not trip over its hem. In her other hand, the basket of produce swung with the momentum of her stride. Her heavy breathing made her lungs feel raw due to the chilly air. When she finally reached the convent, breathless, the midwife was already there. Pilar sat on a small footstool by the bed. For a few minutes, she panted and wheezed louder than Ana Lucia, who was already in labor. When her breathing began to return to normal, she reached a freezing hand to take Ana Lucia's, sweaty and hot, but soft.

Pilar began to sing softly, nervously, to her.

Ana Lucia trembled, and screamed in pain.

Isabel Cristina, now that the midwife and Pilar were finally there, allowed herself to feel shaken. She stood meekly by the doorway with a pale, bewildered face, staring into the time-worn room, as she watched the scene unfold.

On a good day, Ana Lucia could not understand simple instructions. In this agitated state, it was useless to try to encourage her to wait to push when the contractions came. Ana Lucia would tire quickly, pushing when there was no use. Her hypotonia, low muscle tone common with her condition and sedentary lifestyle meant she was generally weak anyway. These births were always precarious, very touch and go.

The father of the child could not have known the risk involved. It's probable that a human being capable of such sexual assault wouldn't care anyway, Pilar had often reasoned. Each time, a delicate life was in danger before even being born.

Sister Pilar continued to try to comfort Ana Lucia, who dug her fingernails into the wood of the bedside table and wailed. Both Pilar and Isabel Cristina, who was still in the doorway, carefully watched the midwife's face. After she had arrived, washed and prepared, she had begun to work. Her expression, at that point, was one of concentration. After several, exhausting hours, her countenance began to change. The midwife was too preoccupied to hide her growing concern.

The birthing had reached the critical stage where Ana Lucia would need to push, but despite the gentle encouragement and repeated attempts to communicate through gestures and soothing tones, neither the midwife nor Pilar could convey that to her. It was doubtful she had the strength anyway. With each passing moment, the baby's distress grew, and the midwife knew they were running out of time.

The convent was miles from the nearest hospital. An emergency cesarean section was out of the question. The baby's position in the birth canal was precarious, and without the mother's active participation in pushing, the risk of asphyxia or severe complications loomed large.

Seconds felt like an eternity as the midwife fought to maintain her composure, her hands trembling as she felt the baby's faint, irregular movements. Pilar could hear the uneven pant of the midwife's breath mingling with Ana Lucia's cries. The weight of what was at stake felt like it was pressing on Pilar's chest, too. The midwife had been silent up to now. Suddenly, panic set in, and the midwife hysterically shrieked,

"Holy Mother of God, please, please!

Isabel Cristina's body jolted, startled by the midwife's abrupt cries.

The midwife continued,

Intercede for this child! Saint Joseph, protector of families, Saint Anne, holy grandmother, help me, help me now. Lord Jesus, have mercy!

Her pleading screams were so loud that they pierced Ana Lucia's own. The walls practically rang with reverberation.

Something in those loud cries reached Ana Lucia. Suddenly, a surge of determination flashed in her eyes.

The midwife's hands were supporting Ana Lucia's abdomen and guiding her, but her voice, now more quietly, continued anyway. She begged with each exhale,

Do not let this baby die in my hands.

Guide me!

Not yet,

Please…"

Seeing that the midwife was in distress, Pilar took over rhythmically coaxing Ana Lucia to push with every contraction. The next few minutes were a disarrayed daze, then miraculously, the baby was there, delivered, red-faced and crying. A healthy, tiny life, breathing on its own against all odds. The relief in the room was palpable as the midwife handed the baby to Sister Pilar. Isabel Cristina, still visibly shaken, stepped forward with a tentative smile, her eyes filled with tears of relief. She had never witnessed a birth before.

Everyone was exhausted, but a healthy boy was born. A beautiful newborn, whose mother did not know she could hold him in her arms. All three infants were born with Ana Lucia's eyes, but this child looked different from his siblings.

As the baby's tiny cries began to echo in the small room, Sister Pilar experienced a tumult of emotions. She felt relief at the infant's safe arrival mingled with a deep, apprehensive dread. She whispered a prayer of thanks and of empathy, knowing that this innocent baby boy had been thrust into a world he did not yet understand, his origins far more complicated than most. It made Pilar uneasy to know that the child's future, like the two born before him, would be arranged by others long before he could speak for himself. His fate seemed to pre-date his very existence.

With Pilar's thoughts far away, the midwife occupied, Ana Lucia now moan-crying woefully, and Isabel Cristina still jittery, joy wasn't immediate. Instead, the sensation gradually penetrated the tension, like a waft of delicious cooking might emerge through a lunch room, taking over the stale air in a dull office.

When Sister Pilar let out an unconscious sigh of relief, tears began to flow openly from Isabel Cristina's broad and innocent eyes. She believed a miracle had just occurred before her, and was completely mesmerized by the newborn child. So much so, that she forgot to pray to God in gratitude.

Pilar held the baby close, preparing herself for the inevitable separation that she knew was to come. He was clean now, and quiet, sleeping peacefully, cradled in her arms.

Ana Lucia had been thoroughly washed and changed, and was finally calm. In her exhaustion, she slept in silence, snoring softly.

Isabel Cristina remained exactly where she had been standing, her gaze never leaving the baby, felt a deep, unspoken bond forming. She silently vowed to protect and care for the infant as long as she could.

CHAPTER THREE

vigil

The dim glow of the single prayer candle on Sister Pilar's nightstand cast flickering shadows on the walls of her small, sparsely furnished room that night. She folded her habit carefully over the wooden chair beside her bed, its coarse fabric rustling softly. As she switched off the same lamp she had each light, Pilar felt that the room was swallowed by darkness this time.

She settled under her threadbare blanket, the crisp, cold air from the open window brushing against her skin. She was so breathless from the day that it took her three tries to blow out the candle. She closed her eyes.

But she woke constantly to every sound.

No one came.

Finally, around 5:45, hours after the man on the old bicycle usually arrived, she heard a door creak.

The familiarity of it caused her to sit upright in her bed, startled. It was the large, wooden door to the convent itself. A door she had triple-checked to make certain it was locked before she went to her room for the night.

The man on the bicycle had never come to the front entrance before.

Hands trembling, Pilar hastily donned her undertunic, a robe, and a pair of socks. She purposely left her shoes behind, so as not to make the slightest sound. She stepped into the hallway, then turned the corner to the main corridor. The moonlight, and a few candles that had not yet flickered out, were the only illumination. They cast long, dull shadows.

In the dim, pre-dawn light, she could see a man's figure, large and indistinct in the faint light. He was inside the convent, walking through the hallway!

The almost imperceptible sound of the intruder's quiet footsteps on the worn, colonial tile floor, was the only sound that broke the silence as he entered the room where the baby slept. Pilar watched, motionless, stunned.

The man was in the baby's room, and Pilar could hear nothing. She stood completely still, trying to detect any sound, wondering if she should cry out for help. She could not hear blankets rustling. There were no infant cries, no footsteps, no movement at all.

Keeping her back to the wall, she slid along the hallway until she was next to the room's door, leaned against the doorway, and peered inside.

Standing, motionless, looking down at the sleeping child was Father Rafael, his back to her.

She felt her throat close. Nothing in her body understood it. Rafael was not supposed to be there. There was no circumstance in which he could possibly be. She retreated, sickened, afraid, and concealed herself several feet away, on the other side of the dark hallway. Her thoughts raced.

Several minutes later, the sound of Father Rafael leaving the baby's room startled Pilar. From the darkness, she watched his movements. They were deliberate yet hushed. His arms were empty.

The baby was not with him.

The heavy, oak door to the convent creaked again as it swung open, and a cool draft swept through the corridor, stirring the night air. Her tunic clung to her shins in the breeze. She waited, then began quickly tiptoeing in the direction of the baby's room even before Rafael had fully, softly, closed the front door.

There the tiny child was, asleep.

Back in her bed, she lay on her back trying to make sense of what she had witnessed. It took quite a while for her heart to stop pounding. Her temples hurt.

In what felt like an instant, her eyes opened abruptly to morning light filling her bedroom. She must have dozed off. Almost six o'clock! She had missed the vigil. If she hurried, she could still make morning prayer. What to say about her whereabouts during the only vigil she had ever missed, well, Pilar would worry about that later.

She rushed off to the Lauds.

CHAPTER FOUR

inheritance

Pilar felt slightly dizzy as she rose from the kneeler, not from the lack of sleep, but from the weight of obedience. It was mid-day and prayers were completed. Steadying herself, she crossed the courtyard. The grass was dry now. It would be a hot day.

Back inside, the hallways of the convent were unexpectedly quiet. A meeting was in progress. Mother Constanza had been informed that the baby was still inside the convent. They all struggled for meaning, but the circumstances would not arrange themselves into any sort of sense. In the end, there was clearly no conclusion to be reached, so it Novitate Isabel Cristina volunteered to care for the newborn while the sisters would try to find out more. Everyone agreed. While the professed sisters continued their busy days, it was helpful that Isabel Cristina was there to attend to the baby.

The nuns had another important matter to discuss during the meeting. They had noticed that Sister Pilar's health seemed to be deteriorating. Although she continued to sing beautifully, her subconscious choices of hymns had become rather dark and sad. Instead of singing of praise, the nuns heard about the death of Christ and the devil himself. It seemed now that every day, their dear Sister Pilar looked so very tired. Her fellow nuns cared deeply for Pilar, and her reputation at the Convent was spotless. They would forever cover for her whenever she forgot to fold linens or wash lettuce and tomatoes. Their message to Mother Constanza was one of genuine concern, and the Prioress took it as such.

In the days that followed, Isabel Cristina developed her own daily routine with the baby. Her routine quickly became second nature. She bathed the baby with care, the scent of lavender soap mingling with the warmth of freshly washed towels. The soothing hum of her lullabies provided a comforting backdrop. As she dressed and fed him her soft, rhythmic coos and the infant's contented gurgles filling the space with a tender, peaceful ambiance.

She would call him Santiago. It was a name of a boy she had known in school. Her classmate meant very little to her, but she had loved the sound of the name.

With no one in her own life to love, Isabel Cristina's bond with baby Santiago would continue to deepen.

The nuns worried. Any day now, the child could be claimed, and they feared that Isabel Cristina would be saddened by the loss of tiny Santiago. The longer he stayed, the more they all dreaded that inevitable night when someone arrived in darkness to remove him from that place. On the other hand, the novitate seemed oblivious to the risk of becoming close to the boy.

And days, then weeks, went by. Still, nobody came. Not the man on the bicycle, not a single soul.

Friday came, the day of confession. On that day, the nuns always walked together up the hill, past the white cemetery gates, beneath the new Cristo de Yungay statue, and across the courtyard before arriving at the cathedral.

Once inside, they performed their rituals, then seated themselves in the last pew with their rosary beads.

The confessional felt stifling and warm that day. It smelled of last Sunday's incense. Pilar took her seat and waited.

There was a long silence before the wooden screen slid open.

"Bless me, Father, for I have sinned," she said quietly, the words catching on her tongue. "It has been... some time.

Rafael said nothing at first. She could hear his breathing, steady but strained.

"Proceed, Sister," he finally said.

"I have allowed my thoughts to dwell on things not meant for me."

"Yes," was his reply. It was an unusual answer. Not exactly encouragement for Pilar to continue. Hollow in tone. She wasn't sure what to do next. She hesitated.

In that moment, something came to her. Rafael had secrets of his own. She had nothing to lose.

"I have judged others. Even those in robes."

"And who are you, to judge?" Rafael's tone was clipped now. "You, of all people, know the danger of pride."

"Yes," she whispered. "We do."

Another silence. She spoke again as Rafael shifted in his seat on the other side of the screen. He had caught the enallage.

"We seek to obey," she said plainly, "but some truths refuse to remain silent."

The screen closed without warning.

Pilar remained seated, unsure if the ritual had ended. No words of penance were spoken. No prayer assigned. Just a final, echoing click of wood on wood.

She rose quickly and smoothed out her habit. Standing alone in the confessional, she recited her own prayer. Then she nodded once, at no one in particular, opened the door and stepped out.

At the convent, several nuns were preparing the evening meal. They spoke in low voices as they set bowls on the wooden countertop, removed husks from corn, sliced bread, filled tiny wooden *cuencos* made of Palo Santo with salt, and gathered other ingredients. Pilar tied an apron on and joined them.

Others had heard the front door open and close during the pre-dawn hours that night.

It seemed to them like countless times that they had stood, forming tortillas in the wooden press, wondering about it.

Sister Pilar casually explained that she had been taking walks at those times.

Now, there were beautiful grounds around the convent in which one could take a stroll. But it would have been quite a coincidence for Sister Pilar to take her first ever pre-dawn walk the morning the baby had been born. Besides, she had been exhausted after the difficult delivery.

Even more mysterious, unless the nuns were receiving guests, they exclusively used the back doors. Why would Pilar use the main door, which had been kept locked for months due to the increased security after the three sexual assaults on poor Ana Lucia? The back doors were locked too, yet they were easier to open from the inside, and more convenient than the main door.

It didn't make sense, but they nodded in agreement anyway. They wanted to believe her. Sister Pilar would never understand why she felt the need to cover for Father Rafael. *As a priest, there was nothing wrong with stopping by to check on a newborn baby, right?* Pilar's own thoughts irritated her. *But why in darkness? Why in secrecy?*

Maybe she felt she owed him at least that, after the conversation they had earlier that day.

Meanwhile, Isabel Cristina's daily routine of bathing tiny Santiago, clothing him, feeding him and playing with him continued.

CHAPTER FIVE

servitude

Whatever it was that allowed Constanza to remain nonjudgmental, kind, and supportive in difficult moments had been shaped long ago. The newly appointed Mother Superior was deserving of the title. She admired Sister Pilar's unwavering loyalty and agreeable nature. She was not simply a Prioress. She was a friend.

She agreed with the others that there was a growing despair in Pilar, and it concerned her. To effectively help a woman like Pilar, Mother Constanza knew, it would take more than idle hand-holding and a pep talk. In all honesty, she didn't know how to approach the issue. Her prayers about the matter did little to clear her mind.

In the end, she decided to schedule a meeting between Sister Pilar and Father Rafael. The three of them had been friends since childhood. Maybe he would be able to come up with some kind of approach to help Pilar.

Gusts of wind rustled trees and bushes as Pilar arrived at the cathedral just before the appointed time for her meeting with Father Rafael. It was a weekday, later in the afternoon. The place was nearly deserted. The large, vaulted cathedral was hushed and cool, the air heavy with the faint, lingering aroma of candle wax from the morning mass. The large chandeliers had all been switched off. Sunlight streamed through the stained-glass windows, casting vibrant, fragmented patterns on the cold terrazzo floor. Pilar made her way to the office, feeling uneasy, wholly misunderstood, and slightly nauseous. The office door was closed, and she could hear voices inside. She sat outside and waited.

Sister Pilar had dreaded this meeting and had prayed for the right voice, the correct approach. It was true, the constant, obsessive thoughts had driven her to a dark place in the past few months. A mental space in which she had never been.

Mother Constanza couldn't have known that Rafael was the source of most of it. Sending Pilar to him for guidance felt like forced penance, although she was certain it was not.

She and Rafael had been especially close for as long as either could remember. Had she not been a nun and he a priest, he was exactly the kind of man she had always imagined would make a good husband. All of that seemed far away now. Pilar felt as though she didn't know him at all.

She was ashamed that her pride, her ego, would not allow her to open up to Rafael about the many things weighing heavily on her heart. She decided she would speak to Rafael as if narrating someone else's sorrow, giving an unfocused account to the priest, strictly in obedience of Mother Constanza' request.

As she continued to wait, she idly wished she was meeting with anyone other than Rafael himself. There was nothing Rafael could say in the conversation they were about to have that would provoke Pilar to express her true emotions. This meeting would be useless.

The door opened. Pilar could hear laughter from both men, and a deacon stepped out.

"Father will see you now," he said to Pilar.

Father Rafael was seated at his freshly polished desk. He smiled and invited her to come in and have a seat in one of the simple, wooden chairs across from where he sat.

Father Rafael greeted her with the well-practiced grandiosity of an experienced priest loved by his congregation. An over-emphasis on warmth and friendliness, coupled with a dose of religious narcissism. It carried a common undertone among clergy:

You have been enthusiastically greeted by me, Father Rafael, so I have done my job and you can go home feeling blessed, knowing I have acknowledged you.

But his friendly smile faded as he took in Pilar's stoic facial expression and uncharacteristically flat tone of voice.

Even though she had obsessed over the meeting all week, even as she waited outside Rafael's office, with minutes to go until they were face to face, suddenly, all the plans she had made didn't seem right in the moment.

In an instant she would later regret, Pilar momentarily set her feelings of obedience to Mother Constanza aside. No matter what the outcome, she would still be a nun, and he a priest when the meeting was over. So, she spoke.

"Father Rafael, I do pray for answers but I'm struggling to find them. I beg the Lord for forgiveness, but the doubts remain," she began. "I know God's plan is not for me to understand. I realize this has nothing to do with me."

"Still," she continued, "I simply can't stop thinking about that baby. Why, this time, did nobody come to claim the child? Shall I tell Elena about him?"

"Pilar!" Rafael shouted, startling Pilar more than just a little bit. "You are right about one thing. This is God's plan! Sister, you must not involve yourself in matters that do not concern you."

In all the years she had known him, Pilar had never once heard Rafael shout. She had heard enough, nodded abruptly, and rose to leave though she had not been asked to. Father Rafael mumbled something about Pilar needing to pray the Rosary about this as he willingly saw her to the door.

Pilar felt more guilt and shame than ever. The Father was right. Of course. This was none of her business. She pushed away her nagging belief that Rafael was the baby's father. She had said too much.

In one way, her prayers had been answered. The meeting was over.

It turned out, in the Divine Mercy Convent, in Yungay, Peru, at that time, there were two residents suffering an existential crisis.

Not only was Sister Pilar struggling with thoughts she could no longer ignore. Isabel Cristina was too. Caring for Santiago made her wish for motherhood even more than a life honoring the vows she was preparing to take.

Isabel Cristina knew Mother Constanza would never allow her to take Santiago with her. So, the darkness that night would have to hide another secret.

CHAPTER SIX

terms & conditions

The first heat and light of the day began to emerge over the mountaintops in the distance. Isabel Cristina kicked up dust as she walked with Santiago on her hip. Eventually, she reached the house she hadn't called home for months. Her mother had sadly passed some years before. The remaining years she spent there with her father and two brothers had been far from pleasant. Grieving the loss of her mother, the three men demanded that she cook and clean, and were generally cruel to her.

It was the reason she had joined the convent.

She paused nervously at the front door; instinct told her not to simply enter, but to knock instead. Her father opened the door. His face was a mix of surprise and irritation as he struggled to understand. His daughter stood at the doorstep holding a baby on her hip. Why was Isabel Cristina not at the convent?

It took some effort to explain to Señor Ysla who the child was. She spoke to her father in the doorway for quite some time before it occurred to either of them to go inside. There was something about his daughter and this unknown baby that felt alien to the man.

The conversation stopped. Señor Ysla stared for a moment, then shrugged and gestured for her to come inside. He would allow it for a while. He liked the idea of having his daughter there to cook and clean again. Still, he was furious she had left the convent. If she was caring for a child, how would she work? Even worse, marriage was probably not an option now. Even though his only daughter was still a virgin, she had a child with her, a son. They were not well off. This situation was only sustainable for a while. Two more mouths to feed would be a burden.

Señor Ysla decided he would try to find a husband for his daughter, one who would also accept the baby boy.

Isabel Cristina had a kind face, smiling features, a graceful gait, and silky, reddish-brown hair. Her naturally caring, easygoing personality meant she had been popular in school. None of that mattered now. *No man will want her now*, the father believed.

He wasn't wrong. Even as word spread through Yungay that her father wished to find a suitor, no one asked for her hand in marriage.

This continued through the beginning of the year. The first few months, they were met with heavy rainfall almost daily. Baby Santiago was healthy and thriving. However, Isabel Cristina's father's patience was growing thin. She would endure a slap for a spill, an overcooked meal, or an unmade bed.

She took each smack with bravery. She reminded herself it was for Santiago. She remembered the vows she had been learning at the Convent while she was there. She would pray, and pledge to do better.

May came, and the rains began to taper off. The hilltop park had been brightly decorated for the Fiesta de las Cruces. There were crosses covered in fresh flowers. Colorful fabric and banners ran the length of the entire courtyard. Crowds gathered around. With fascination, they peered into small, painted wooden boxes called Retablos. Inside each box was an intricate, miniature scene of religious or folk life. Each box was surrounded by colorful flowers and beads on woven string.

Isabel Cristina walked slowly around the park, with Santiago wrapped in an *aguayo*, which was in turn wrapped around her back and shoulders. He was still light to carry. It seemed the whole town was there, and she enjoyed it immensely. As it grew darker, the cathedral lights were ethereal as a backdrop to the scene. Still, she stayed only until the first lanterns were lit, then she made her way down the hill. It was not a long walk home, but Santiago had already fallen asleep. Her father and brothers stayed behind, sipping Mezcal as folk musicians began to play nearby. She hummed along to the music, even when it grew distant. When she could no longer hear it, she made up melodies and lyrics of her own, and smiled as she looked down at the *aguayo*. Life was hard, but as long as she and Santiago were together, Isabel Cristina was at peace.

The Fiesta de las Cruces had a unique way of bringing the town together. Old, young, rich, poor, and everything in between. They all partied alongside one another until the early morning hours.

Exhausted from walking all day, she slept soundly and was not awakened by the arrival of her father and brothers. Santiago slept through the night as well. In the morning, she woke early. There was no smell of tea coming from outside her bedroom door. That meant her father must still be asleep. She tiptoed out of the room, past the sleeping baby, prepared a bottle for him in the kitchen, and snuck back into her bedroom, gently closing the door.

Sun began to warm the room through the sheer curtains. She scooped the baby up into her arms and sat on the edge of the bed. Santiago held the bottle tightly with his lips, enjoying the cool milk and the warm sunlight. He was still in her arms as she leaned back against the wall.

She had just closed her eyes when there was a loud knock at the door. The baby jumped in her arms, his small arms waving reflexively, but he didn't cry. He was too preoccupied with his bottle to care.

Before she could get up to answer the door, she heard her father open it promptly. When did he get up? She hadn't heard him, and he had been out late the night before, partying at the festival.

She heard a booming male voice greet her father,

"Yslaaaa." the voice resonated, too loud for the tiny space.

Unsettlingly, with this man, her father adopted a meek and humble tone. Isabel Cristina heard her father respond to the man with the utmost respect. It was odd.

A few minutes later, her father tapped on the door to the room where she and Santiago sat. She shifted the baby onto her hip, still latched onto the bottle. Opening the door, she looked out. She saw Don Fernando, and two others, seated at the table. The Don sat sideways in the chair, impatiently tapping a sealed cigar on the tabletop.

Her father entered her bedroom and sat down. He looked dejected, beaten.

"Look, Isabel…" he drawled.

She could already tell this wasn't good news.

"I have tried; I honestly have tried my best. I am out of options. You will take the child and live in the servant's quarters, and work for the honorable Don Fernando Javier Alarcón on his ranch.

Señor Ysla crossed himself as he spoke the name. It was out-of-character for him to be so reverent. Father and daughter stared across the room at one another blankly.

"The other servants will care for the baby while you work. When he is old enough, he will work too. There is no pay, but all of your needs for food, shelter and clothing will be met. In time, I'm sure you will make friends with the others who live there. It's not so bad. You already know it is one of the most prestigious ranch properties in all of Yungay. The hacendado is here now, to take the two of you there."

Isabel Cristina inhaled, then held her breath for a moment, thoughts racing. *A life of a servant! Awful? Yes. At least Santiago would accompany her.*

The irony was lost on her that Santiago would be living on the same property as his half-brother and half-sister. They would be living lives of extreme privilege. He would be a slave.

The men who had come with Don Fernando left the house while she gathered her things, numbly. She felt rushed. When she was ready, she walked out into the kitchen, where her father and Don Fernando waited.

She led the way out the door, not making eye contact with her father.

As they walked up the hill to the hacienda, the Don looked her over. He did not offer to help carry the baby or her belongings. They made their way through an iron gate.

A man in a neat butler's uniform waited for them in the meticulously manicured gardens.

"This is Rumi. He will take you to your room." Then, he turned, still speaking. They watched him, coughing as he disappeared up the path, his shoes clacking on the flagstone.

CHAPTER SEVEN

running water

Isabel Cristina's throat was tight, and she was flushed with hot anger as she glared at Rumi. She felt like she had just been traded, or handed off like property. Rumi didn't seem to notice. He absentmindedly gestured toward a single-story adobe building not far away. She followed as he began to walk toward it.

It consisted of several small private rooms and a large shared area in the center. This was to be her new home. The thin door swung open. Several people made their way through the doorway, the middle of a lively conversation, carrying heavy wooden tubs filled from the well.

At least my father's house has running water, she thought.

Rumi sat down, and leaned back. The small chair looked like it might snap in half under his weight. He looked bored, as if he had done this countless times. Casually, he introduced Isabel Cristina to a petite, elderly woman. "This is my mother, Maria," he said. "Everyone calls her Ama."

Ama's face was deeply lined, not with bitterness, but with time. Her skin had the warm tone of sun-aged earth, and her dark eyes, though rarely lifted, missed nothing. Her silver-streaked hair was always pulled back in a simple braid. She was dressed in all black, which was traditional for widows in that time.

Ama smiled and bowed slightly. Then she gestured toward a doorway. Isabel Cristina studied the tiny, sparse room she and Santiago would share. She walked slowly. Isabel Cristina could tell by her frail frame that she was no longer capable of laborious tasks.

Rumi, Ama, and the rest of the servants spoke in an ancient, indigenous language. Quechua dialect filled the house. She understood only a little. Rumi explained that none of them had been to school. Only two of the servants spoke Spanish.

It took only minutes for her to settle in. She had few belongings. She studied the room. A metal bed with a thin mattress. A small crib. A three-legged wooden table once painted a bright aqua blue. Hardly any paint remained. On top sat a small lamp. A rosary dangled from the switch beneath the metal shade. The beads were dried coffee beans.

She turned, and left the room, holding Santiago, and took a seat nervously in the common area. Rumi was waiting. He sat opposite her. She felt calmer now, so she studied his face. Wide eyebrows, high cheekbones, and the face of a butler. Rumi wasn't friendly, but came across as fair, approachable and helpful. He spoke quickly.

His mother Ama, he explained, had once been the personal maid of Doña García. The highest-status role for a woman on the ranch, he added, with a hint of pride. The new arrangement would be that Ama would watch baby Santiago while Isabel Cristina worked.

As Rumi spoke, she glanced at Ama. Something about the woman's calm presence told her Santiago would be safe in her care.

Santiago did not sleep well that night. Not wanting to wake the others with his cries, Isabel Cristina spent most of it sitting upright in bed, holding him.

In the morning, the servants' house was bustling long before dawn. There was a plump, middle-aged woman with a short braid. Rumi explained that she was the chef. Two younger women, who appeared to be in their twenties, shared one of the rooms. Both had silky, straight black hair, but one was taller and paler than the other. They were sisters, one a maid, and one a kitchen helper. There was also a nanny, she was told, who slept in the hacienda, to be close to the children, but shared meals and the little free time they had with the rest of the group.

She had not finished giving Santiago his morning bottle when it was time to leave. He cried helplessly as he was handed over to Ama, who would finish the feeding, wash and change Santiago.

Rumi instructed Isabel Cristina to report to the dining room, where the Doña would be waiting for her.

She stepped outside. An older man with weathered skin walked an old, black bicycle toward the servant's quarters. He was tall and still strong. A boy, pale and pimply, maybe sixteen, accompanied him.

Rumi called out from the doorway.

"Introduce yourselves."

Obediently, both stopped. The younger one spoke in broken, street Spanish.

"Hello, ma'am. I am Leandro," he said proudly, pointing at his chest.

"...I heard you went to school! *My* teacher was the city herself," he apparently felt compelled to share. "I'm an orphan. I survived on the streets of Yungay, but I got in trouble a lot. The local police finally got tired of me and convinced Don Fernando to take me on as a ranch hand."

"This is Don Nazario," he continued, gesturing respectfully to the older man. "He's in charge of *all* the animals and the grounds here. I work for him."

Leandro grinned, as if he were second-in-command to someone important.

"Some say Don Fernando was lucky to get me for free, but I've got a roof over my head, shoes on my feet, and food to eat..."

In the doorway, Rumi interrupted.

"*Chico!*" he bellowed, then continued in Quechua, "The young lady is expected in the hacienda by Doña García. You must allow her to be on her way."

Leandro looked disappointed. "And you should be getting back to work," Rumi said sternly, but with a smile.

Nazario gestured for Leandro to follow.

"Nice to meet you, ma'am," Nazario said with a nod. The two disappeared toward the woodshed. The bicycle leaned against the wall.

Isabel Cristina continued up the hill, toward the ranch. Children played on the lawn outside.

At the hacienda, Isabela fought the urge to study every detail of the grand dining room. It was all she could do, standing in the midst of such luxury, to look Doña García in the eye and focus.

As she spoke, Doña García studied her with a peculiar gaze. Although she was awestruck, and a bit shaken, she could see that Doña García's face was oddly playful, as if she had just received a new toy.

"You have been to school, and I understand, spent time at the Convent." Doña García said, after looking at Isabel Cristina for several seconds. Her voice was articulate and her inflections regal. Isabel Cristina admired her.

"What a blessing that you and I will be able to communicate."

The Doña didn't speak Quechan at all. She looked at her husband.

"Yes, I will use her."

Don Fernando nodded once, turned and left.

The two women stood, facing one another. Doña García paused, pressed her hands together as if in thoughtful prayer and spoke.

"All the uniforms we have here," she said, "are Ama's size."

Ama stood barely four foot nine.

"In the morning, be ready to accompany me into town," the Doña said. "We will visit the seamstress."

She had never ridden in a car before. Rumi pulled up in a beige 1967 Chevrolet Bel Air.

Hundreds, maybe even thousands, of cars had passed her as she had walked along the roads in Yungay, yet she had never seen a car like this one.

It was angular and sparkling. The outer portion of the rims were painted to match the car, and the insides were shiny chrome. The interior was tan, with dark brown piping and accents.

Rumi motioned for her to sit in front, next to him. They drove up the circular driveway in silence, where Doña García stood with her children, waiting.

She kissed the young boy on the forehead, while the nanny gently untangled the girl from her tight clutch on her mother's skirt. The Doña warmly assured them both that she'd be back soon, then carefully arranged herself in the back seat with practiced regality. As she smoothed her skirt, the car pulled away. The engine was quiet and the ride was smooth.

As the car descended from the hilltop toward town. Isabel Cristina stared out the passenger side window in wonder. Everything looked different from this perspective than it did from the road's edge.

Her thoughts were interrupted by Doña García's voice coming from the back seat.

"My dear," she asked innocently, "how did you come to be the caretaker for the beautiful little boy?"

Señor Ysla had already made clear to Don Fernando that the child was not his daughter's. They understood that.

She didn't know how to respond.

"His mother is a woman who is pretty, but disabled. She can't care for him, and his father never came to claim him," was the best she could manage.

This seemed to satisfy Doña García. She was quiet after that.

At the seamstress' shop, a woman brought out several bolts of fabric and laid them on a large table. Doña García selected fabric for an ankle-length gray cotton dress. She would pair it with crisp white linen, to tailor an accompanying apron and head scarf.

A small group of servants stood together in the distance as the car made its way back up the driveway later that afternoon. They watched, as Rumi stopped the car at the main entrance. He got out, curved swiftly around the gleaming hood, reached for the passenger side rear door and opened it with a wide, swinging motion. He extended his hand and helped Doña García, who stepped out gracefully.

Hearing the car approaching, the two children raced out of the house excitedly. "Mamá!" they shouted. She knelt and embraced them, then the three headed inside.

Rumi moved the car to the front of the coach house, and turned off the engine. As Isabel Cristina stepped out, the servants looked on, in awe. She had ridden in the car! They marveled at how the Doña had personally shown her around the ranch, and started to train her. How lucky the girl was to be the recipient of so much of the Doña's individual attention. They could hardly communicate with the Doña, due to the language barrier, so they understood and simply accepted it without envy. To them, and to Doña García, it was a given. Isabel Cristina would rise quickly through the ranks, and fill the void Ama had left when she became too elderly to be the Doña's personal maid.

At that moment, her place within the group was affirmed. From that point on, she was treated with the utmost respect.

After that, life at the ranch did not seem so bad. She spent her days inside the hacienda. She avoided the heat. She fetched no water. Her only concern was Santiago. He would not be spared from hard labor as he grew older. Ama sometimes stared out the window, worry on her face. Isabel Cristina guessed she must be thinking the same thing.

A week later, the uniform was ready. The Doña arranged for only the dress to be collected, sending the apron and headscarf to a local woman for embroidery. Intricate blue flowers would line the apron's hem and the edge of the scarf that would frame her face. Doña García chatted excitedly about it. Isabel Cristina waited with anticipation to see it.

The first week passed. She was quickly learning the Doña's routine and was beginning to be able to anticipate her needs without her mistress needing to ask. In the evenings, she would spend cozy nights back at the servants' house, playing with Santiago. He had begun to smile and laugh.

Each day, she made the short trip between the quarters and the hacienda. She delivered laundry, returned with fresh linens. Each time, she noticed Ama watching her.

CHAPTER EIGHT

encumbrances

The only known, living relative Ana Lucia had was her sister Elena. Unlike Ana Lucia, Elena had been born neurotypical. Her life, apart from growing up with a disabled sister, had been relatively uneventful. At nineteen, Elena had married Antonio, a young man from Huaraz. Situated near the Cordillera Blanca mountain range, Huaraz was a bustling city compared to Yungay, the much smaller town where Elena and Ana Lucia had grown up.

Elena and Antonio owned a home there, and a car. They had built a comfortable life in her new hometown. It had been nine years since Elena had left Yungay. She made a point of visiting her sister twice a year, never missing a trip despite the discomforts of the long and rugged journey. Their parents had passed away, and these visits were the only family connection Elena had left.

Elena had no children, so she had once believed she and her sister would be the last in the family line. The first two mysterious births had haunted her, changed her. Somewhere out there, she had relatives. Nieces or nephews. Since then, she couldn't escape a constant feeling of hollowness she hadn't had before.

Her untimely visit took place while Isabel Cristina was still working at Don Fernando's ranch.

The trip was particularly arduous due to the heavy rain. Elena normally traveled with her husband. This time she came alone, due last-minute commitments he had in Huaraz. As the bus slid and bounced unsteadily, close to the edge of the road, high in the hills, she tried to comfort her uneasiness by telling herself she had faced worse conditions, but the inclement weather still made the journey slow and grueling. The bus finally pulled in to the station around noon on Wednesday.

She was tired, but relieved to finally reach the convent. Ana Lucia's limitations had never stopped Elena from adoring her sister. Over the years, she had also formed a strong bond with Sister Pilar. She was looking forward to seeing them both.

Pilar had been weighing her options, and decided it would be best if Elena visited Ana Lucia first. Then, she would tell her.

She made small talk with Elena, as they approached Ana Lucia's room. It wasn't difficult, since Pilar genuinely liked her. Upon hearing their voices, Ana Lucia moaned agitatedly in recognition.

Only two things could calm Ana Lucia. One was Pilar's singing. The other, her sister Elena's voice as she held her hand and spoke softly close to her ear. Elena's voice was warm, as she recounted every detail of her life since their last meeting, speaking as if Ana Lucia could understand each word. Even though Ana Lucia was incapable of responding, Elena treated her with the respect and intimacy of family, believing that if there was any chance she could grasp her meaning, she deserved to hear them as a whole person, her sister.

This time, it took longer to calm her. Pilar had already noticed more restlessness in Ana Lucia this week. Elena remained patient, as always. Her sister's hand wrapped around hers, her gentle words in her ear. Finally, she sister was comfortable. The painful wailing gradually subsided. Elena continued talking, her voice now the only sound in the small room. Twenty-five minutes later, Ana Lucia was asleep.

Elena always felt a rush of loneliness as she left her sister's side. She would cherish the memory of each visit until the next time they were able to spend time together. Still, she felt even worse for her Ana Lucia. She suspected that these moments of connection could not possibly leave the same lasting impact on her sister as they did on her. She felt it was deeply unfair, and wished there was more she could do, some memory she could leave with her until the next time. The weight of that realization made Elena leave her sister's room in tears every time she said goodbye.

Seeing Elena's tears, Pilar lowered her head and looked at the floor. The worst, she knew, was not over. The remainder of the visit would be difficult. Pilar's private prayers had already become pleas, her faith wavering under the weight of her doubts. Each word she whispered felt hollow, her once-unshakable belief now eroded by the darkness that had seeped into her soul. Twice, she had watched as pieces of her rosary fell to the ground, loosened by the wear of anxious fingers.

When Elena last visited, nobody had realized yet that Ana Lucia was pregnant. That day, Pilar not only faced the excruciating task of telling Elena that her sister had been raped a third time. She also needed to share the heartbreaking news that Elena was now an aunt to a newborn nephew she would never know. Pilar understood that the news she would share that day would be devastating, especially given Elena and Antonio's struggles with infertility.

Even worse, Pilar knew nothing about the child's whereabouts. Elena tried desperately not to pepper her with questions, her agonizing search for answers winning out in the end. Pilar understood. She answered patiently, trying to hide the hurt inside.

The two women looked at each other as their tea grew cold and went unfinished. Elena went back to the bus station and sat on the bench waiting, watching. Everyone there was a stranger, yet they all looked familiar to her. A child that resembled Ana Lucia when she was just a young girl. A man in the shadows that resembled her brother-in-law. A mother with an infant.

People looked different in Huaraz.

On the bus, Elena stared out of the window, in silence. What a tragedy this birth was for Ana Lucia. And for her.

Sister Pilar returned to the table where the two had been sitting. The half-empty teacups were still there. She sat for a while, then slowly stood up and began to clear the dishes.

CHAPTER NINE

there anyway

Isabel Cristina's second week at the hacienda was busy. Everyone was involved in the preparation of a dinner party on Saturday night, on top of their regular duties. Normally, half crews worked Saturday and Sunday to allow the servants some time off. Not that weekend. After their day's work was finished on Saturday, everyone would make final preparations for the party. On Sunday, they would clean up.

Late Saturday morning, the Doña summoned Isabel Cristina. The last pieces of the uniform had arrived. It was complete. She followed the Doña's hand as she gestured toward it, neatly pressed, on a hanger, draped over an upholstered armchair in the salon. The Doña walked over, looped one finger around the hanger's hook and lifted it gleefully to show her, suppressing a girlish giggle.

They were the finest garments she would ever wear.

They had arrived just in time. The guests would be arriving soon. Isabel Cristina returned to the servants' house, quickly washed and changed. Ama helped her to tie the apron neatly behind her back and comb her hair. Then, she hurried over to the hacienda. The party would be starting soon.

The guests stepped in with rustling silk and polished shoes, ushered by Rumi. They were greeted obsequiously by Don Fernando and diplomatically by his wife. They positioned themselves in the parlor, decorated with colonial furniture and ornate chandeliers on the high ceilings, mingling before dinner.

Isabel Cristina emerged from the kitchen carrying drinks and small appetizers on a tray. Doña García was entertaining several elegant women. The gentlemen had separated into smaller clusters. Don Fernando stood near the fireplace, speaking in hushed tones to another prominent landowner.

Even among all of the finery of the room itself, and the glamour of everyone in it, Fernando's role was unmistakable. His presence was the epicenter, with the perceived respect, piety and righteousness of everyone in the room. Their envy could be seen in his eyes as he commanded attention with practiced élan.

She stood still, balancing the tray, considering who to serve first. *Ladies first?* She thought. *The people closest in the room? Yes, maybe that would be best. I don't want to pass by them to serve others...*

Before she had finished her thought, her eyes met Don Fernando's. He looked straight at her and abruptly stopped talking to his companion. Both men stared at her, beautifully dressed in her new uniform. The Don gestured for her to approach them with the drinks she carried, which she obediently did. She felt his gaze on her body.

Hours later, the servants' house was dark, as she finally approached it, exhausted. Moonlight poured in through the open slats, so she didn't need to bother with a light. She took off the uniform with the utmost care and collapsed into bed.

She was so tired that she didn't notice the empty baby cot on the other side of the room. Santiago had been sleeping the full night for quite some time now. She assumed he was there, asleep. Why wouldn't he be?

When she had come into the cottage, she also hadn't seen Ama, who was sitting, hidden in a dark corner. Ama was holding Santiago, who was fast asleep in her arms. Don Fernando didn't see Ama either, twenty or so minutes later when he entered the cottage, a bit uneven in his steps, and passed as quietly as he could to enter Isabel Cristina's room.

Ama rose. She walked outside with the stealth and silence of a nocturnal pampas cat, baby in arms. She managed to get far enough away from the doorway that Santiago did not wake as Isabel Cristina's screams echoed through the courtyard. A loud clatter followed, and Ama watched as the young woman ran out into the night, trying frantically to pull her clothes on as she sprinted away from the servants' house.

She ran as fast as she could through the flagstone courtyard, right past Doña García, who looked pale as she stared blankly at the scene unfolding in front of her.

The Doña was close enough to stop her, but she did not react. Isabel Cristina saw the light of the distant hacienda light up the woman's cheekbones in the darkness as she sprinted by.

Back at her father's house, Isabel Cristina paced in the dark. She could think of nothing but Santiago, abandoned by her, alone at the servant's house. Would Don Fernando dare retaliate against a baby?

She glanced at the closed door of her father's room. Everything was still. She could hear her own breathing.

Her father's internal alarm clock had always been the sunrise. At dawn, the door opened, and he walked out slowly, ruffling his hair. Then he saw her.

She looked flushed and windblown. She had not slept. Señor Ysla stared, mouth open. She tried to explain, but her words came in stutters and fragments. He understood nothing.

Hearing the two of them, her brothers' bedroom door swung open, and they rushed into the room, looking concerned. As the story unfolded, the shock on all three of the men's faces gradually turned to terror. Don Fernando would undoubtedly come searching for her there first.

It made sense. She shuddered at the thought of an inevitable visit from that disgusting man. She could still smell his horrible breath, a putrid mix of *lomo saltado* and Chianti, with a distinct reek underneath.

As quickly as she could, she searched for any belongings still at her father's house. There wasn't much. Most of what little she owned remained in her room at the servants' quarters on the estate. She found a scarf that had belonged to her mother, and a cloth shopping bag. Her father went to a clay jar in the kitchen, and emptied what was left of the *maíz tostado* (dried corn) into the tote, nourishment for the journey.

She took a long drink of water before stepping out into the sun, which was now warming up quickly.

Years ago, when her mother was still alive, the two had visited a strange shop in a remote part of town; a mere shed behind a Chapel. One of the few possessions of value in the Ysla household was a small, framed photograph of unnamed ancestors from her mother's side. The gilded surface of the frame had begun to crackle. Señora Ysla had heard that the woman who owned the shop might be able to restore it.

Inside, before even looking at the frame, the shopkeeper first studied young Isabel Cristina for an uncomfortable few moments. She was barefoot, a worn deck of cards in front of her. She spoke quietly.

"Everyone has two zodiac signs," she said. "Girl, the sun is inside you, and the rising sign that meets the world. Tell me, what is your birthday?"

Isabel Cristina answered the woman, more out of obedience than curiosity. She felt mildly afraid of her.

"And the time of day you were born?"

She looked to her mother, who answered for her.

The woman lowered her chin. Her eyes drifted. Then, with a voice softer and farther away:

"You, *querida*, are a Pisces. With a Cancer rising."

Isabel Cristina squinted, wrinkled her nose.

"This means you have a heart that breaks for others. A heart you won't know how to repair. But it will mend, always. Not through strength. Through something beyond you."

She tilted her head back to rest against the wall and looked at Isabel Cristina, eyes half open.

"Some are made of stone. You are made of cloth. Cloth is also strong, in its own way. People will trust you with their secrets. Even their lives. And nothing that happens to you will be planned."

After that day, Isabel Cristina would recall the woman's words from time to time. Over the years, less often.

That day, as she ducked onto side streets, making her way across town, that memory came to mind once again. This time, she felt as if she would finally understand. As she walked, she constructed and reconstructed it, comparing it with the events of the past twenty-four hours. But there was nothing conclusive to be realized, no insight to be had.

With nowhere else to go, she returned to the Convent.

Convents are good at this sort of thing. For centuries, during wartime and peace, times of political unrest or, as in Isabel Cristina's case, personal persecution, convents have provided sanctuary to those who have needed it when others failed to do so. Mother Constanza, Sister Pilar and all of the others had quite a bit of experience with people seeking asylum.

Even when she was safe inside, Isabel Cristina still whispered to them in fear. She shook as she recounted the events of the last twelve hours.

The nuns were mostly relived. They had lost sleep, prayed, and worried endlessly about the disappearance of the two of them a few weeks before. They sprang into action, guiding Isabel Cristina to a cellar underneath the kitchen, where she hid among crates of potatoes and mesh sacks of vegetables. The air smelled of onions and rust from a boiler. The thin ceiling creaked with muffled footsteps and she could hear indistinguishable conversations from the kitchen above. She listened to the voices, terrified that one of them would be Don Fernando's. But she heard only nuns.

The cellar had a high, tiny window that provided a bit of daylight. She had helped the nuns make a blockade a few feet away from it by stacking up old boxes and crates.

There was just enough space for a little light to still shine through, yet no one could see much of anything inside. After they were finished, she sat alone on an old, discarded table in the opposite corner of the room and waited. She longed to hold Santiago. It was the only thing that might comfort her.

She was safe for the moment. Still, they all knew the situation was sustainable for only the shortest period of time.

Don Fernando's people did come. On his orders, they aggressively tore through Señor Ysla's small house, searching everywhere. They even read his mail. Then they proceeded down the block, banging on every door, demanding that the neighbors tell them if they had seen the young woman. But nobody would admit to such a thing, even if they had.

Not finding a shred of evidence that the young fugitives had been there, they moved on to the Convent, where they knew she had been living prior to her arrival at the ranch.

They asked questions, threatened and made demands, but they didn't get past the front door. The nuns cooly refused to respond, and they were turned away.

Don Fernando didn't dare go to the police.

It wasn't the law he feared. He knew his status as a wealthy landowner and his ability to pay off officials would all but guarantee him immunity from any charges. Rather, it was the gossip. He couldn't risk the public embarrassment if word spread. Already, there would be talk of his men ransacking Isabel Cristina's family home.

Señor Ysla was not wealthy, but he was respected. People would wonder what provoked him to do such a cruel thing to a man with lesser means than himself. It was assumed that Ysla's daughter was still working at the ranch, which would confuse them even more. When it came down to it, Señor Ysla's word would be trusted over Don Fernando's.

And what would happen if someone from the town asked Isabel Cristina why she was hiding?

He needed to keep this quiet, and find the girl before she could damage his reputation.

Back at the convent, Mother Constanza remembered that as a novitate, Isabel Cristina had been assigned to Sister Pilar. The two of them had seemed to get along, so she asked Pilar to come up with a plan.

Sister Pilar dutifully arranged for a soft mat, pillow, blanket, jug of water and glass to be sent to the cellar. Then she began gathering details.

There was a teenage boy who managed his own father's floral stand in the marketplace where Señor Ysla bought his vegetables. All the flowers at the cathedral came from there. That would mean the two passed each other every day. Pilar hurried to the hilltop and waited for the day's delivery.

Not long after she arrived, the young man walked, whistling, pulling a wagon up the pathway. It was full of flowers.

Sister Pilar met him at the doorway of the cathedral and helped him carry the pots inside. As they worked, she asked him for a favor.

The next day, the teen returned with an abbreviated version of the story as relayed to him by Señor Ysla. As usual, their paths had crossed in the marketplace. The boy had lifted a potted flower and extended it toward Señor Ysla, pretending he was trying to interest the man in the plant. The ruse allowed the two of them just seconds to speak, in the most hushed of tones.

The boy told Sister Pilar that Isabel Cristina had been offered the servant position by Don Fernando Javier Alarcón only after her father's attempts to find a husband for her had failed.

If Sister Pilar had not been such a holy woman, she would have burst out laughing. *Couldn't find a man? For such a lovely young woman?* She thought, amused. You see, that's what Nuns do. Marry people off!

She handed the boy several coins and a piece of sweetbread wrapped in wax paper, and thanked him with a smile.

Returning to the convent, Pilar made her way to the common room. Devotion was over, and it was not yet time to prepare the evening meal, so she thought she might find Sister Dolores there. Dolores had a nephew in the military. He would know many young men from far beyond Yungay.

Later that same afternoon, Pilar had a suitor. Isabel Cristina borrowed clothing and cleaned up for the visit. Curtains were shut tight so that passers-by couldn't see inside. She came upstairs only long enough to meet the young man. He was sworn to secrecy and not given her name.

The man had a strong build and a thin face. He spoke softly, and appeared slightly nervous. Isabel Cristina was equally shy, so Sister Pilar asked most of the questions. Typical things, like what the two enjoyed doing in their spare time, how many children they would like to have, and so on. The interview didn't go badly.

The young man left and Isabel Cristina returned the clothing and returned to the cellar. By the time she was settled, Sister Pilar was attending her devotions. It would be a few hours before the two would have an opportunity to talk.

When Pilar was finally free, she descended the stairs and turned the corner into the cellar. She was surprised to find the young woman sitting on the ground, clutching her knees. She had expected her to be preparing for an immediate departure. Their eyes met briefly, then Isabel Cristina lowered hers with a guilty look.

"Please forgive me, mi reverenda *maestra de novicias*," began Isabel Cristina in a low voice, using the title Sister Pilar had once held for her. "I cannot marry that man."

It was that moment that broke Sister Pilar. Pilar had not cried in about twenty-five years, and yet there it was, a hot tear running down her cheek. Her newfound doubts about Father Rafael, her recent state of mind, the horrific, multiple sexual assaults on Ana Lucia, her guilt for not trusting God's plan, and her desperate wish to protect Isabel Cristina from a horrible fate if Don Fernando should find her... it was all too much for her to take. Pilar was facing an existential crisis that would haunt her for the rest of her life.

It shocked Isabel Cristina to see Sister Pilar weep. "No, *Maestra*, please don't worry so much. I will marry him."

She believed Sister Pilar's tears were solely concern for her own safety.

Pilar collected herself. "No." she said softly, shaking her head. "Please rest for the afternoon, I'll ask another of the devoted to bring you a hot meal." Pilar straightened her body slightly. Her voice trembled. "Excuse me. I will go to pray for the wisdom to make a new plan."

News within the Convent that Isabel Cristina had rejected the suitor spread fast. The next few days, everyone at the Convent was on edge. Nuns bickered. Some felt empathy for the girl; others were frustrated and insulted that she flatly refused to cooperate. Any sound caused the nuns to react nervously. What if news of the spurned suitor traveled back to Don Fernando? What if he showed up here, in person, demanding to see her? What if he shoved his way past the nuns into the sacred Convent? How could they stop him if he did?

Isabel Cristina couldn't force herself to care. She could not stop thinking about baby Santiago. She missed him intensely.

Faced with starting over, Sister Pilar went back to work following the order Mother Constanza had given her to sort something out. Pilar knew she needed to balance spreading the word far and wide, with utter secrecy.

Not an easy task. After weighing what seemed like every possible option, she finally decided that the best course of action would be to phone her cousin in Trujillo. The distance between the two cities would slow down the process, but would nearly guarantee that the search for a husband for Isabel Cristina would not reach the ears of Don Fernando.

The Convent did not have a telephone. Sister Pilar made her way to the cathedral offices to make the call.

Pilar's cousin, also a nun, resided in the convent of Trujillo in the same order as the Divine Mercy Convent of Yungay. Pilar made the call on a Saturday. Her cousin was immediately fascinated by the story and eager to help. With religious services taking place over the weekend, it would be Monday before the search for a suitor in Trujillo would begin.

Tuesday came, then Wednesday. Thunderstorms over Yungay lasted most of the day. The cellar where Isabel Cristina still hid was cold, and growing damp. Time passed slowly. Sometimes, she paced, sometimes she wept. She thought constantly of Santiago's tiny fingers, his face, the way his cheeks wiggled as he drank his bottle.

Still no word from Trujillo. Shame set in, and for the first time, she felt afraid.

CHAPTER TEN

departures

After days of waiting, a young man arrived at the convent. Sister Pilar recognized him as one of Father Rafael's new Deacons. He relayed a message: She was to telephone her cousin in Trujillo. The nuns thanked him with warm rolls. He and Pilar set off toward the cathedral offices, huddled under a single umbrella. His wet vestment slapped lightly at their heels in the wind and rain.

Pilar's cousin had good news. They had indeed found a suitor. A bus trip from Trujillo to Huaraz, then another to Yungay, would mean travel through mountainous and rugged terrain. The journey would be long and challenging. Road conditions were poor, due to the recent heavy rain. Pilar's cousin had generously convinced the local parish to give the young man bus fare. He would travel as soon as he could.

Time seemed almost at a standstill. The overall air of anxiety at the Convent did not change. It was not until the following week that the Deacon came again. This time, he said, no long-distance return phone call to Trujillo was necessary. He was simply to tell Pilar that the passenger was en route.

Which, he was. But he arrived in Huaraz late, after the ten-hour journey. There were no more buses leaving for Yungay that night. His journey would continue in the morning.

Isabel Cristina, remembering Sister Pilar's tears of disappointment, slept very little. She prayed that she would not again look blankly at her suitor, feeling no connection, as she did the last time. From a humble prayer-state, she drifted into harsh thoughts of self-condemnation, believing that perhaps she should have just gone along with the plan, even if she felt nothing for the man. The cellar was cold, and thunder rumbled outside.

Finally, late morning the following day, there was a knock at the door. Pilar had closed all of the curtains two hours before. The Convent was still under strict security due to the assaults on Ana Lucia. Now, they had a hidden refugee in their midst as well. A man waited on the doorstep. He could hear movement and whispers inside. The nuns rushed off to find Sister Pilar.

Pilar came to the door. Before sliding the latch completely free, she asked a few identifying questions through a small opening. When the young man confirmed he was from Trujillo and gave the name of Pilar's cousin, he was let in. Isabel Cristina, tired but dressed in borrowed clothing and ready for the visit, came into the room and joined them.

"Good afternoon," the young man began. "I am Esteban Felipe Córdova."

He was charming, without question.

Sister Pilar, and likely many of the others, prayed vigorously that evening, thanking God. The couple were to marry in the morning, and get out of town as fast as possible.

For that reason, the tiny ceremony carried a particular air of relief. It was decided that using the cathedral would be too risky under the circumstances. The deacon's presence was plausible. He had already visited twice. Father Rafael's would have been harder to explain. With Rafael's delegation to the deacon, the pair were married in the convent's prayer room.

There were no rings. Just two nuns as witnesses, and no reception. Isabel Cristina's family was secretly notified, but they didn't dare attend in case Don Fernando's men noticed and followed. The groom's family and friends were far away, in a distant city on the other side of the mountains.

After the ceremony, the newlyweds were to board the next bus to Huaraz. At the convent, Sister Pilar sat on the edge of her bed, her rosary in hand but idle, quietly taking in the relief.

Isabel Cristina had another plan.

It was nearly dark. The newlyweds set out on foot to the estate of Don Fernando Javier Alarcón, or more specifically, the servant's house there.

They approached a low stone wall surrounding the adobe structure. The air was warm and dry. Inside, there was silence. The servants had all left the common area and retired to their rooms for the night. Isabel Cristina and Esteban crouched low, behind a chicla bush. She gave him a nod and they approached the courtyard.

Every so often, a leaf or dried berry dropped from the tree above and landed on the corrugated metal roof with an almost inaudible thud. The glassless windows were tightly shuttered for the night. Outside, they passed the large brick oven, which was still slightly warm. Baskets lined the walkway on either side, ready to be collected in the morning as the servants rose before dawn and returned to work.

Isabel Cristina slid away the simple wooden latch on the front door and stepped inside. She recognized the lingering smell of traditional Quechua food from the evening's meal. The room had not changed. A poured-clay molded Christian cross still hung on one wall; some simple stools, but no chairs; a few belongings and an extra blanket or two on the floor. Nothing more.

In the sparse room, it took only a second or two for their eyes to adjust. She quickly located baby Santiago sleeping in a small cot. She picked him up. His eyes opened wide in surprise, and he let out a loud cry.

The servants awoke instantly, startled by the noise. It was too dark for them to recognize Isabel Cristina, and they had never seen Esteban before. To them, both were intruders. They began to scream in Quechua. Esteban stepped back in surprise and knocked over a stool.

The servants' fear quickly turned to confused looks when they recognized Isabel Cristina, but there was no time for explanations. She tightened her grip on Santiago, and they made their escape.

Had it not been for the unfortunate circumstance that Don Fernando was enjoying a pipe on the porch of the hacienda nearby, they would have easily gotten away.

Nothing like this had ever happened on the ranch, and Fernando instinctively knew there was trouble. He grabbed his shotgun. The servants were, after all, his property. The ranch could not function without them. He rushed to investigate.

Inside the servants' house, the situation was chaotic. The servants were in the midst of an argument in Quechua, debating what should be done. The only acknowledgment Fernando received was a couple of glances in his direction. He turned and hurried out the door.

Back behind the chicla bush, Isabel Cristina and Esteban were waiting silently for the chance to run. The rustling of a thick layer of leaves and sticks on the ground would make escape impossible. But if they waited, they would be discovered quickly.

A twig crackled under their weight. Without a target, Don Fernando fired his gun in the direction of the bush. The bullet clipped Isabel Cristina's lower leg. She let out a cry, and baby Santiago was thrust from her arms as her knees buckled. He landed hard against the bush, gashing his arm on a dried branch.

There would be no story ever told about Esteban's exceptional courage that night. Instead of retreating, though he knew their location was already obvious to Don Fernando, he pulled hard, trying to drag his new wife and baby Santiago to safety.

"Go, please. Just run," Isabel Cristina begged him. Although they had only just met, she did like him.

Yet Esteban stayed. He still tried bravely to move the two of them. As he did, Isabel Cristina's leg left a trail of blood in the dirt. He pulled for as long as he could.

At the last possible second, when Don Fernando was almost upon them, he hurled himself back behind the stone wall and watched in horror.

In all the commotion, Don Fernando didn't realize there had been two intruders. His eyes flickered with cold detachment as he leveled the shotgun. He looked down at Isabel Cristina in disgust. Three more gunshots rang out, echoing in the still night as she crumpled to the ground, still clutching the baby's blanket. From the ground nearby, he scooped up the shrieking baby and disappeared back into the darkness, with the blood of both Santiago and Isabel Cristina on his clothes.

Esteban would never know why Don Fernando killed his new bride. Inside the hacienda, Doña García had heard the gunshots. So did Ama, from within the servants' house. In the morning, they learned the deceased was Isabel Cristina.

It was the quietest day ever at the ranch.

In the silence, Doña García and Ama each studied the face of Don Fernando at separate times. There was nothing to be understood from his countenance. To them, his face looked as it always had.

By the time the Don understood there had been two intruders, Esteban was far away, heading back to Trujillo alone. He was poor, and therefore inconsequential to men like Don Fernando, or even to a poorer man like Isabel Cristina's father, Señor Ysla. Even their wedding had been a non-event, protected by the nuns' secrecy. Esteban left no legacy behind that anyone had lived to tell. At any rate, he rationalized, Isabel Cristina was forever silenced and the child was still in his possession.

Ama and the servants attended to Santiago's wounds. They were deep and took a long time to heal. There would be scars, but the child was otherwise fine.

CHAPTER ELEVEN

souls

A tragedy like this was exceedingly rare in Yungay.
News travelled quickly. Father Rafael first visited Señor
Ysla to deliver the sad news, then walked to the Convent,
where he gathered the nuns. Sister Pilar watched his face
as he spoke.

Father Rafael was somber as he spoke of the murder of Isabel Cristina, which he presented as "accidental" to the group. After all, he justified aloud, Don Fernando, a major benefactor, didn't know he was shooting at *her*.

When he spoke of baby Santiago's near kidnapping, and the minor injuries the child had sustained in the process, his voice trembled. He paused. He dabbed at his eyes.

Pilar's utter horror turned to coldness as she studied Rafael.

She *did* feel for Santiago. Of course she did! But Isabel Cristina had been shot. Not injured. Killed.

A newlywed, robbed of a life.

And now, here was Father Rafael, moved to tears over a scratched infant and offering soft explanations for the man who had taken aim in the dark and fired at a young woman, ending her life.

Were they truly equal, Isabel Cristina's murder in cold blood and the cuts on Santiago's arm?

Or worse, was Santiago's survival the greater loss in Rafael's eyes?

Without turning her head, she glanced around at the others. No one seemed to question the priest's words.

Pilar's hands had gone numb in her lap. Her fingertips were white, and her rosary beads pressed into her skin. She didn't unclench.

A funeral was arranged. With his usual solipsistic grandiosity disguised as selflessness, Rafael made a show of granting Pilar his permission to use the cathedral phone to call Elena, although he didn't quite see the point. Privately, he wondered why they would care about Isabel Cristina's death. He rationalized that Pilar was grief-stricken and probably wanted to be surrounded by anyone who could bring her comfort.

Anyone who truly knew Sister Pilar would have easily recognized that she would never burden others in that way.

What had horrified Pilar just kept getting worse. *How could Rafael completely forget that Elena would be Santiago's biological aunt?*

Rafael's attention quickly shifted to the preparations. The phone call had been made. Not that it mattered much, he told himself. Even if Elena didn't attend the funeral, Pilar and the rest of the nuns would find comfort in the large congregation he expected that day.

The word in the community was that nearly the entire town would attend. That would mean a large audience for his eulogy, and a big day for the cathedral's coffers. He scooped up his notebook and a pencil to begin drafting his homily.

He walked toward the courtyard, where he usually did his writing, without another thought of Pilar or Elena.

Three days later, the organist played the first chords as the service began. Isabel Cristina's sweetness and charm, and their shock at the tragic nature of her death, had brought people from near and far. The cathedral was packed.

Don Fernando and Doña García were there, seated in the second pew behind Señor Ysla and Isabel Cristina's two brothers. This was not an event Fernando would normally have attended, but he felt his presence conveyed his innocence and grief over what he referred to as a "tragic accident."

He had, however, forbidden any of the servants from attending.

As Father Rafael was about to step up and begin to speak, the doors swung open one last time. Elena and Antonio, both dressed reverently, walked in. Bus service had run late, but they made it. They seated themselves in extra chairs that had been placed along the back wall for an overflow of guests.

"In the name of the Father, the Son, and the Holy Spirit. Amen."

Rafael's voice echoed off the chandeliers.

"Dear brothers and sisters, we are gathered today to commend Isabel Cristina to the mercy of God. We entrust her soul to the Lord, who does not abandon His own."

CHAPTER TWELVE

incense & ashes

Isabel Cristina had been laid to rest. Parishioners brought roasted *cuy*, *papa a la huancaina*, *choclo con queso*, and cornbread. They served it with *chicha de jora*. The community center was filled to capacity. The crowd, dressed in black, was a visual reminder that this was a somber event, even as occasional laughter could be heard.

Amid the sadness and tragedy, friends and family who had not seen each other in far too long were reunited. It was just as it is at most funerals.

That was particularly true for Elena. It felt good to be back in her hometown, even if the circumstances weren't ideal. She had known Señor Ysla since his family moved to town when he was a boy.

Antonio seemed content to be eating and talking about soccer with a group of men, so Elena took a moment to approach Isabel Cristina's father, and offer her condolences. She hadn't heard about his wife's passing. Now, he had lost his daughter too.

Señor Ysla greeted Elena warmly and seemed to genuinely appreciate her kindness. He reached out to shake her hand, but he didn't let go. He glanced nervously across the room at Don Fernando and his wife. They seemed occupied, deep in conversation. Then, he pulled Elena toward him and whispered something in her ear.

After dinner, Sister Pilar led the remaining group in song. It was as if an invisible, heavenly scale balanced the intense sadness of the day with the beauty of the weather and scenery around them in the same, beautiful hilltop park where the Las Cruces festivities had been just a few weeks before.

The sun set in the Andes. Elena and Antonio were given cots for the night in the cathedral's rectory. In the morning, they rose and made their way to the convent.

There, Elena held her sister's hand tightly and wept. She was emotionally drained, yet grateful to have unexpectedly seen her sister a second time during the dry season. The conflict of emotions left her exhausted. Ana Lucia didn't moan for long. Elena loosened her grip on her hand as she fell asleep.

Sister Pilar was in the kitchen, wrapping leftovers from the large meal the day before in butcher paper, before carefully arranging them in an empty cookie tin.

"Take these for the ride home," she said to Elena and Antonio. "And before you go, I've made you some *mate de coca* to calm your nerves for the long journey."

There was a small, rugged wooden table in one corner of the kitchen. Although there was a grand dining table in the adjacent room, this smaller one was used more often by the nuns for quick meals. The three gathered there. Sister Pilar prayed in memory of Noviate Isabel Cristina, for the safe travels of Elena and Antonio, and to express thankfulness for the food and drink she had just prepared.

The *mate de coca* was still too hot to sip.

Elena pressed her lips together, then spoke quietly. "Before we leave, there's something we'd like to talk to you about," she told Sister Pilar.

Pilar's eyes opened, soulful and wide. She placed one open hand on her chest. "Dearest in Christ, Elena, please do know of my devastation and utter sadness that your sister had once again been taken advantage of." I deeply regret not being more honest with you."

There was silence. They both stared at Sister Pilar. Pilar's voice cracked as she spoke, and she looked as though she might begin to cry.

Elena and Antonio glanced at each other, disoriented. Then, Elena gently touched her other hand, which still rested on the table. Pilar had misunderstood.

"Sister, that's not why we're here," Elena said softly, blinking. "We both know how devastated you are that Ana Lucia was once again violated in this way. We know you did everything you could. We're not here to blame. We're here because we need your help."

Sister Pilar bowed her head and took a breath, collecting herself. After a moment, she looked up and her eyes met Elena's once more. Elena noticed the confusion in her brow.

She continued. "Sister Pilar, Antonio and I continue to pray. Still, we have not yet been blessed with even a single pregnancy."

"Yesterday, I found out the identity of my sister's third child. It is the child, Santiago, who Isabel Cristina took with her to the ranch of Don Fernando. It is the boy she died trying to rescue from a life of slavery there."

Hearing those words spoken out loud for the first time startled Pilar. They disoriented her, as if someone had just entered her private thoughts. Her round face was pale and she looked exhausted as she pieced it all together.

Naturally, Elena and Antonio want to take custody of their biological nephew and raise Santiago in their loving home. With living relatives to care for him, he never belonged on a ranch being trained for a life of slavery. He is not an orphan. His mother is alive. Ana Lucia is Elena's sister, and since she can't care for her child, they want to.

Her thoughts were correct. They earnestly asked Pilar to help arrange a meeting with Don Fernando Javier Alarcón and his wife to discuss the matter. They assumed the logic would be clear.

Sister Pilar assured them she would try. She attempted to hide the doubt in her voice.

After Elena and Antonio boarded the bus back to Huaraz, Pilar rushed through her chores so that she could spend extra time in devotion that afternoon. She arrived twenty minutes before her normal prayer time, knelt, and closed her eyes tightly.

Time had passed. Her burden was not lighter. *Why, why... had Rafael done what he had? Why leave the third child there, abandoned?* Worry had settled into Pilar's being and now had a permanent place within her. She felt like it never left her, even during prayers.

She had thought joining a convent would mean servitude and goodness. Instead, all Pilar felt was the weight of other people's lies. *Why did I listen to Rafael? I wanted to tell Elena about her nephew. I wanted to tell her about all three of them. What made me silent? Would it have been a sin to tell the truth? It feels now like a sin that I didn't.*

Isabel Cristina's bravery had given Pilar hope. It was bitter and cruel to imagine Santiago waiting on his own half siblings just a handful of years from now. *Why did Don Fernando have to take Isabel Cristina's life?* Her death seemed so unnecessary. *Wouldn't a beating or strict punishment have sufficed?*

She knew instinctively that a meeting between Don Fernando, Elena and Antonio would likely not go well. *What incentive would Don Fernando have to surrender Santiago?* He saw the child as his own property, a valuable asset. *Who, in Yungay, would challenge that?*

Yet, Elena and Antonio were now the child's last hope.

CHAPTER THIRTEEN

the unredeemed

It surprised no one that Don Fernando was against the idea of giving Santiago to Elena and Antonio. Ever hopeful, the two made three separate trips to Yungay, once in treacherous weather. Sister Pilar diligently scheduled each of the meetings.

Not only was he firmly opposed to surrendering the child, he also refused to allow his wife to be present for any of the meetings. Pilar suspected that Doña García would have taken a softer approach, especially knowing that Elena was Santiago's aunt, and that her husband knew it.

All three meetings were a waste of time.

There was never a moment when Don Fernando even briefly considered letting Santiago go. As he rejected them again and again, he looked as though he rather enjoyed toying with them. He had the habit of leaning back in his chair smugly, idly playing with his mustache, watching them like a predator prolonging the chase, savoring the inevitable end.

Even when they offered a substantial sum of money, Don Fernando coolly refused. He was already wealthy enough. Besides, Santiago's value over a lifetime of indentured servitude was worth far more to Don Fernando than any amount Elena and Antonio could afford to pay.

After each meeting, Pilar sat quietly with the couple in the convent. Elena would visit Ana Lucia, which gave her time to recompose herself. As they left, she would cheerfully say, "See you the next time we are able to schedule a meeting with Don Fernando."

This time, Pilar didn't have to study Elena's face for long to understand the woman was defeated. It came as no surprise to her that Elena's farewell was, "We will see you when we visit Ana Lucia next time," instead.

For a brief moment, there had been hope for the child. As long as Elena and Antonio were talking to Don Fernando, there was a tiny chance the ending might be different. Now, nothing was left.

It was that desperation that pushed Pilar to move forward. There was no other way out. A life was at stake.

Father Rafael was surprised to discover a note on his desk requesting an afternoon's leave from Sister Pilar. In all the years he had known her, she had never made such a request. Aside from a three-day illness some years ago, she had not missed a single day.

With the request granted, Sister Pilar went about her devotions in her usual way on the morning of the meeting. She was surprised they didn't feel much different than on any other day.

As midday approached, she soaked in a bathtub, neatly combed her thick hair and tucked it up into a braided bun at the nape of her neck.

Then she walked. Sister Pilar's Sunday habit, freshly laundered and pressed, hung crisply on her frame, the dark fabric free of blemish or wrinkle. The simple white wimple framed her face, its edges perfectly aligned. Her face was clean, confident, and serene. Her veil, always plain and modest, fell neatly down her back.

The cobblestones of the city gave way to freshly leveled dirt paths as Sister Pilar continued, small basket in hand. This one time, she did not sing as she walked.

She carried a handwoven pair of white mittens with red and black woolen needlepoint at the cuffs. There were peaches and avocados, perfectly ripe. Also, *turrón de Doña Pepa*, a traditional sweet pastry made from flour, sugar, and honey. Pilar never asked for anything. Nearly anyone in the market community would happily donate whatever she asked.

The landscape around her shifted from rural to manicured. Pilar made her way past the iron gate, through the flagstone courtyard of the Alarcón ranch and knocked on the carved front door of the hacienda. She could hear the two children laughing inside. A young female servant answered.

Isabel Cristina's replacement, Pilar guessed. She was not as kind-looking, but roughly the same size and stature.

"May I please see Doña García? She is expecting me."

The servant stepped aside.

The two women had the finest of afternoons. Doña García accepted the gifts with sincere gratitude. They drank tea and enjoyed one another's company. Although they had not known each other well, every time they had met in the past, their personalities had connected in a quiet, unmistakable way.

Later, the Doña played the piano while Sister Pilar sang. It didn't matter what melody she chose; Pilar knew the lyrics to them all.

When the visit was over, Pilar asked if she could briefly meet with the Master of the house on her way out. She lied, nervously. She told Doña García that she had a message from Father Rafael to deliver to her husband. What other plausible explanation could there be?

Don Fernando had just returned from town, where he'd met with his banker. He received Sister Pilar in his office, still dressed in street clothes and slightly flushed from the sun.

He sat behind a large, carved wooden desk with inlaid shell designs. Everything about the room was exquisite. The long drapes were the color of rich sangria. Thick woven rugs echoed the same deep hues, their patterns carefully chosen to match. It looked as though every detail had been considered by an interior decorator. Sunlight poured through the sparkling clean windowpanes.

Sister Pilar took a seat in front of the desk and began slowly.

"There have been incidents where an individual has entered the sacred Convent, sir. Our disabled resident, Ana Lucia... forgive me God, as I speak these words... has been sexually assaulted not once, but three times."

She sensed some of the smugness slip from Don Fernando's face. She continued.

"At the time of two of poor Ana Lucia's pregnancies, sir, it was noticed that you and your lovely wife had been lighting candles before mass, praying for children. I do wonder how even the gracious Doña García managed to remain so thin during both of her own pregnancies, and to keep it such a secret from us all."

Don Fernando's face was not flushed anymore.

"But shortly after Ana Lucia gave birth, miraculously, so did your wife," Pilar continued, "after that, your prayers for children ceased. Praise God. I am in awe of how He has blessed you with a family, and with such a lovely wife as well."

At this point, Don Fernando, fully grasping the stealth of the nun's accusation, cloaked as piety and delivered with full deniability, grew agitated.

What is the message you needed to deliver, Sister?" he snapped, angrily.

Sister Pilar smiled piously, just as nuns always do when they know they have done good work.

"The mysterious fate of the two newborns of poor Ana Lucia remains an unsolved mystery," she said. Her tone had shifted from reverent to innocently concerned, another trait many nuns possess: the ability to say the unsayable with tone alone, since their practice forbids them to speak certain truths aloud.

"I understand that each infant was delivered to a man on a bicycle..."

Sister Pilar rose, ending the conversation with no apparent conclusion.

She had seen the bicycle on her way in.

CHAPTER FOURTEEN

kin

Elena and Antonio received a call early the next morning. Don Fernando Javier Alarcón had grown tired of the child. He told them it would be years before Santiago would be strong and capable enough to do any meaningful work on the ranch. His care was taking up too much of Ama's time. It was time that Ama could be spending on more helpful tasks. Besides, Santiago was another mouth to feed.

The Don practically ordered the couple to pick up Santiago by the week's end.

Two days later, Ama and all the other servants were gathered outside the front door of the servants' house when Sister Pilar arrived with Elena and Antonio to collect Santiago. The boy was now two and a half. The servants viewed the toddler as part of their family. He brought what little joy they had in their difficult lives to the only home they knew.

Doña García was unwell. She did not get out of bed that day.

There was an amicable air of respect and gratitude. Even though the servants were sad to say goodbye to the child, they seemed to understand he was going to a real home, where he would belong in a way he never had on the ranch. They knew what Santiago was too young to understand. He was narrowly escaping being trafficked into a life of enslavement.

Ama handed Elena a small blanket that Isabel Cristina had taken from her father's house when she first brought Santiago to live there. Elena looked at Santiago. He was already carrying another blanket he seemed to like better. Elena gestured to Ama to please keep the original. A remembrance of time served, but also time shared.

"For you," Sister Pilar and Elena said simultaneously, in Quechua.

The sunny afternoon grew still. Ama's eyes met Elena's. Ama could tell that Elena understood her mixed feelings, the happiness and the heartbreak in that moment. She bowed her head and accepted the blanket, tears now fully formed in her eyes.

Santiago slept for most of the journey back to Huaraz, his small head resting in Elena's lap. Before they left, Pilar had handed Elena a small bundle wrapped in cloth. It contained food for the trip and a paper packet of herbs to help Santiago sleep. Elena hadn't expected the way her hands would tremble slightly as she took it. The weight was light, but something in it felt important, and final. Pilar had tied the cloth with care.

As she looked at the bundle, she said silently to herself, *Sister Pilar packed that for my son and me.*

Then she looked at Santiago, his eyes closed, resting on her lap, and thought silently once again, *Sister Pilar packed that for my son and me.*

At the house in Huaraz, the adjustment began slowly. Santiago clung to Elena at first, uncertain of his new surroundings. But within days, he began exploring the apartment, and Elena began the work of building a new, secure world around him. She hung curtains, brought home wooden toys from the market, and made stews that filled the apartment with warmth. Each evening, she sat with him on the porch swing. When she sat there before, in the glowing light of evening, she had always imagined rocking a child to sleep in that place.

Santiago had other plans. He would stay wide awake with his head against her chest, quiet and still, as if listening for something beyond sound. It made her smile. Mother and child; their trajectory no longer a filament in her own head. Her legacy had an existence of its own now.

Elena exhausted herself daily in this new role, yet at night in bed she could hardly sleep. There was a quiet energy within her, a kind of joy she had not experienced since childhood. Her prayers had been answered. *Her* child even shared a bloodline with her.

Santiago grew. At school, his flair for the dramatic and witty humor earned him the title *encantadorito*, or charmer. Elena picked up on the nickname. She used it once in a while, with a broad smile, when he would make her laugh.

Her husband Antonio didn't accept the nickname. If he ever used it, it was more with a sneer. He once muttered it under his breath when Santiago sang for guests. Elena pretended not to hear. He felt his son should have a more practical and serious nature. He also believed Elena showered him with too much attention.

Still, times could not have been better. In the beginning, young Santiago was a bit delayed learning to read and write, due to the odd mix of Quechua and Spanish he had heard his whole life. But he had a quick mind, and caught up in less than a year. He won over every one of his teachers; so entertaining and animated, they would say. A caring boy, cheerful, and naturally curious. When the class was asked to draw their families, Santiago drew a picture of Elena with a large sun above her and labeled it *mi mamá*, as if no further explanation were needed.

Elena adjusted the household budget to provide Santiago with singing, dance, and drama lessons. He excelled at all three. His acting and voice instructors had never seen his equal. Such developed skills at such a young age. They viewed him as a prodigy in the world of performing arts. His talent deepened as he grew.

Elena also taught him how to garden and cook, and when he was old enough, she brought him along to the places where she regularly volunteered. Together, they fed the hungry and delivered baskets to families in need during the holidays. Santiago went wherever she did, learning not just by instruction, but by being near her.

They also continued to visit Ana Lucia twice each year.

Even though open acknowledgment of such things was rare at the time, Elena felt that her sister deserved to be recognized for her true role, even if it was for only one of the three children. She explained to Santiago that she was his *mamá*, and Ana Lucia was his *mamá de sangre*.

CHAPTER FIFTEEN

may 31, 1970

Santiago woke on the morning of his sixth birthday and sprinted out of bed, leaving his Bugs Bunny sheets in a pile. The smell baking in the kitchen filled the air. Although he was too young to realize it, nothing meant more to him than awakening to family that day. The thought of getting gifts and treats distracted the young boy from any sentimental feelings. The excitement of the day sent Santiago skipping through the garden, arms wide, dancing and singing.

Suddenly, he felt a firm tug on one of those open arms. Then, a forceful yank spun him around face to face with Antonio.

"If you damage my plants," he hissed, "I will put you to work fixing them like the slave you were."

Santiago never dared mention encounters like this one to Elena. He feared Antonio would become even meaner in retaliation. His uncle had a surreptitious way of making sure they always happened just outside his wife's view.

Santiago put on his jacket and went back outside. After wandering around a little more, he sat down on a low, cinder block wall.

Elena called through the open window. He didn't move. She asked him if he would like a cup of soup. Santiago didn't want soup. He didn't want anything.

"I'll wait for birthday dinner," he said, a little sheepishly. He didn't want to hurt Elena's feelings. It was Antonio he was mad at.

That seemed to suffice. Elena left the kitchen and the backyard was quiet. Santiago laid back on the wall. The sun was warm on his body. He dozed.

An hour or so later, he was awakened instantly. The ground around him shook. There was a low, but loud, rumbling sound as the earth settled. The sound wasn't coming from any particular direction. It was coming from everywhere. It lasted what seemed like a very long time.

Through the window, Santiago could see the lights swaying inside. Then, they flickered out.

Elena rushed outside. She covered his head and shoulders with her hands and upper body, leaning over him in protection to guide him away from danger. Antonio followed. The three of them huddled in the clearing for a while. There was quiet.

When it felt safe again, they rose. Inside, the birthday cake had been in the oven, baking. But the oven was off now. There was no power, no electricity. There would be no birthday dinner, just cold bread and corn by dim candlelight.

Back in Yungay that afternoon, a young mother had felt the same earthquake. Her husband, the baby's father, was away at work. The intensity of it scared her as she watched the adobe walls of their modest home begin to crack around her, and the lights go dark. Frightened, she thought it would be best to get out of the house. She dressed the two of them warmly, grabbed her baby daughter's stroller and left quickly.

The usual daily walk of mother and child brought them uphill and past the cemetery. She rushed along that path, not knowing where else to go. From the top of the hill, she could see the bustling town below. The circus was in town, and the tents were visible from where they stood.

She reached the Christ the Redeemer statue. Gradually, she looked around to see a crowd of almost one hundred people had gathered there in fear, seeking refuge atop the hill like her.

That group, ninety-two people to be exact, looked on in horror as a massive avalanche of ice, snow and rock came rushing down from nearby Mount Huascarán, the highest peak in Peru's Cordillera Blanca Mountain range.

The entire town was buried under ice and boulders as they watched. Utterly terrified, the young mother huddled with her baby, near the base of the statue. They had only a tiny blanket from the baby's stroller and the clothes they wore. The skies grew dark as clouds of dust and debris formed above them.

It would be days before rescue efforts would reach them. The hilltop, with the arms of Christ the Redeemer still outstretched above them, was sacred and hellish all at once. The eerie silence was occasionally interrupted by settling debris. There were many aftershocks. The group could smell the few small fires burning under some of the rubble. They filtered muddy water through clothing to make it drinkable and foraged food from homes and shops buried in rubble.

In Huaraz, time stopped. Santiago, Elena and Antonio sat in their home, still without power after days. They discovered there was no running water, either. They talked to their neighbors over the walls. Nobody knew what was happening.

The skies refused to lighten. The dust clouds would not dissipate. The hours passed slowly. The darkness made reading difficult, and they barely had enough candles to provide light at night. So, they sat and waited.

The following day, Santiago sat idly on the edge of his bed in half-darkness. He clicked the switch on his lamp several times. Still no lights. His room was eerily quiet. He jumped when he heard a loud banging on the door.

Antonio answered. Santiago peeked around the corner and watched. Foreigners in uniforms were delivering water.

"This is the emergency rescue team, here to deliver supplies," a man in a blue hat and uniform bellowed.

Emergency, Santiago remembered. Before that moment, he didn't know that word.

In the house, they had enough food lying around, enough canned goods and bags of dried mote to be safe. But the cupboards were starting to look bare. Antonio and one of the neighbors decided to take the car out and try to find an open fruit stand or shop. They didn't get far. The entire northern portion of the city was unrecognizable. Roads were closed, impassible, with deep piles of rubble everywhere. All businesses were closed, some destroyed, the rest without power. They went back home with a new level of awareness of the devastation.

There had been no word from Yungay. There, many of the small group of survivors still on the hilltop were close to death when humanitarian rescue finally arrived several days later. Those assisting in the rescue efforts searched the highest ground first, hoping to find anyone still alive. The young mother and her daughter were airlifted out along with the others. There were still no phones. Trains were not running. They slept in shelters, until they were finally able to make their way to the young mother's parents' house, who happened to live in Huaraz.

Once the parents had their daughter and granddaughter safely settled in Huaraz, the mother immediately thought of Elena. The two were friends who had met while volunteering. They enjoyed a kind of kinship because they both had grown up in Yungay before moving to Huaraz.

Santiago and Antonio had been bickering all morning. They glared at each other as they watched from the end of the hallway. Elena answered the door. They recognized her friend from Yungay. The woman gestured for her to come outside. The two sat on the porch swing and talked in whispers.

In the house, which had become even quieter now, Santiago made his bed, sat cross-legged on it, and waited. The two women talked for a very long time.

After what seemed like forever, he heard the front door close softly. He took one step outside his bedroom door. He saw Antonio at the opposite end of the hall. No one moved closer.

He would not forget the sight of Elena in that moment. It was difficult to articulate, but she had a thoroughly spooked look, like someone who was appearing very collected, yet clearly was not. Many would look horrific after receiving such news, but Elena had always had more equanimity than most. Still, when she finally spoke, it was with a terrible hollowness only reserved for the very worst.

The earthquake they felt had also triggered a landslide. The reports were searing: nearly twenty-five thousand lived there. Only hundreds survived. Not a single building stood. The statue of Christ the Redeemer the young mother huddled behind still stood at the highest point of the city. Only the top of a single wall of the Cathedral of Santo Domingo de Yungay remained. The rest of the parish of Father Rafael, buried.

Elena hardly slept after that. Three days passed.

Then, before dawn, as she lay awake in bed, she heard movement. The squeal of bicycle tires in their driveway, and the dull thud of a newspaper landing on the front porch. The paper boy.

She pulled on her bathrobe and ran outside, scooping the paper up quickly. Finally, some news.

She sobbed as she read. The destruction was the worst natural disaster in Peru's known history. Like most tragic events with mass casualties, so many were connected to at least someone in Yungay. A large portion of Huaraz was nothing but rubble now. The avalanche had been an enormous force of debris. Glacial ice, snow, boulders and mud. Elena's hand shook as she read that six or seven towns had been buried. Obliterated. Several others sustained significant damage, like Huaraz.

She laid the newspaper flat on the table, then lowered her head and rested her forehead on it, eyes closed. After that, it seemed there was more tragic news every day.

The newspapers made lists daily of the names of survivors, a lot of them children. Fate seemed to mock the disaster in one respect. For whatever reason, the circus tents the young mother had seen from atop the hill protected many children who were inside, and a man dressed as a clown had led them to safety.

Prior to the tragedy, Elena had left the newspaper for Antonio to read first, then she read later whatever interested her before throwing the paper away. Since the tragedy, she had been waking up early. Her first thought of every day was to retrieve the paper and read the names of the survivors.

One morning, she sat at the breakfast table, warming her hands on her mug. The paper reported that foggy conditions were slowing down relief efforts. She looked out the window. One of the pair of small, black wrought-iron chairs was missing a rubber foot. It rocked in a clacking rhythm in the light wind. Looking at it, Elena could tell the visibility was low. It was only a few feet away, yet she could barely see it in the yard.

There would be no rescue efforts that day, but it was the day the power was finally restored. To watch the news on television, which had interrupted all broadcasts and was airing all day, brought the tragedy even more into focus. They showed black and white images of devastation where cities had once been.

To no one in particular, she said softly,

"That's all we have left now, to learn to live with what God sees, even when we can't."

Soon after, the lists of the names of survivors subsided. There were no more names to print. Nowhere left to search. Elena didn't dare hope that the nuns would be able to get a disabled woman out in time, so it seemed almost certain that Ana Lucia had perished. Her sister was gone. Sister Pilar was gone too.

There was simply no town. No Yungay.

CHAPTER SIXTEEN

the last

Sometimes Elena wept, sometimes she shook, and sometimes she was quiet. Pilar's melodies didn't come to her anymore. Ana Lucia's hand was no longer there to hold.

Santiago could hear the silence and feel the empty space.

Elena's endless and beautifully unconditional love for him never wavered, but she was forever different. The rest of Santiago's childhood was calm, but never the same. Peaceful, except the occasions when Antonio felt the need to remind him who he was.

Something had been on his mind. Elena had always been open about Ana Lucia being his *mamá de sangre*. With adulthood looming like a challenge he wasn't quite up for, Santiago began to contemplate what that meant. The house began to feel temporary.

He decided to start saving money. First, it was a newspaper route. Then, a slightly better job stocking shelves at a local hardware store. He grew tall and handsome. He still had a slightly boyish face. The handling of heavy boxes at the store gradually gave him a muscular appearance. Inside, he was still *encantadorito*. Charismatic, outgoing and charming. Unchanged. The childhood nickname still fit.

As a young lady from Yungay marrying a man from Huaraz, Elena had spent her entire early married life proving that she was more than just a "girl from the provinces." She had always been naturally elegant and sophisticated, but she worked hard to continue to refine those parts of her. The charities she was a part of became an identity, particularly because she remained childless for so long.

Back then, she'd stayed busy. It kept her from seeing Antonio clearly. Grief reversed that. Now, her own insides were harder to ignore. She could see clearly the relationship between her son and her husband deteriorating.

Although no one had spoken of it until the time came, all three agreed it might be best for Santiago to move away once he reached adulthood.

Antonio had kept the thin, black, felt-like sheet of protective material they use to ship computers, part of the packing most people throw away. He slid it over his keyboard, and gently closed his laptop.

"Booked. One way ticket to Guanajuato, Mexico," he said, sounding bored.

The nearby city of San Miguel de Allende had a growing reputation for theater and performing arts. So, with a duffel bag, the relatively small amount of cash he had managed to save, and some packed snacks, Santiago set off, alone.

It was still daylight when the plane touched down. As it descended, he saw only brown. So different from the lush greenery in Peru. The air was drier than he expected. He used some of his funds to hire a driver to take him to San Miguel. Almost two hours away, it would be an expensive fare.

He stood outside the small terminal, waiting for the driver who wasn't there yet. Across the street, a painted ad on a wall read *Allí, de todos modos.*

He read it once. Then again. His soul felt like it was on the line.

The taxi honked. He turned, picked up his bag, and crossed the street.

At Elena's request, Antonio had arranged Santiago's first week's stay at a shared group inn. It loosely resembled the youth hostels of today. A popular destination for backpacking young Mexican travelers, the inn was full. Santiago didn't speak much. He wasn't sure how the others would react to his Peruvian accent. He silently slept, hugging his duffel bag tight to his body as he did. The sheets smelled faintly of bleach and old leather sandals. Somewhere nearby, someone coughed in their sleep.

In the morning, he woke to the sounds of many of the travelers preparing to leave. It took him a moment to realize where he was. Santiago gathered his things and ventured out to the nearby central plaza to explore.

Most of the city's architecture was colonial in style. Santiago was pleasantly surprised. He had expected a more traditionally Mexican town. San Miguel was truly stunning. There was a large cathedral, a clock tower and other historic buildings surrounding the open area. The cobblestone streets and colorful buildings felt like stepping back in time. Laurel trees lined the plaza, providing greenery and shade to the hundreds of people gathered there. The place had a warm, inviting energy. Even just wandering around, there was so much to take in. It was like every corner had a story to tell.

Santiago couldn't wait to see more. But first, he needed to find a permanent place to stay. He looked for signs, and asked an elderly gentleman for his newspaper as the man approached the trash can to throw it away. Finally, he arranged to rent a room in the small apartment of a widower. His landlord was a rather unkempt man, and a smoker. The room was dated, worn and utilitarian. It was all Santiago could afford. Still, the landlord had a rudimentary interest in the city's theater arts and could hold a conversation. It wouldn't be too bad.

As Santiago expected, acting didn't immediately pay off. The money he brought with him was almost gone. His landlord suggested he try a local tour agency. They were always hiring guides.

Bookings for local tours were done by travel agents and at hotels. The tour company's office was not a place that tourists ever visited. It was a shabby, second floor, single-room office near the bus terminal with three desks inside. There was no seat for a visitor, so Santiago stood and waited. The phones rang loudly.

He got the job.

Still just seventeen, Santiago was the youngest tour guide at the company. Nobody seemed to notice. His acting experience gave him a big advantage in terms of presentation and professionalism. He soon became a favorite, and the compliments from tourists poured in. It wasn't long before Santiago memorized the history of every monument and the contents of every museum in town.

It was there Santiago met his first friend.

Marco worked in the museum store. At that time, in San Miguel de Allende, it was an exceptional job for a young man. Marco had relatives with connections who got him in the door. Santiago would walk tourists through the gallery, and out into the store, where they would buy coffee table books and other souvenirs. Marco looked well-off, in V-neck sweaters with his slightly longer hair neatly combed back.

Despite his connections, it was Marco himself who succeeded on his own merits once given the chance.

To say Marco was friendly would be an understatement. He exceeded even Santiago's energy in terms of extroversion. Marco was intelligent enough to quickly learn the register, how to process credit cards, and other aspects of the job. He kept track of the new items and made sure he looked them over when they arrived, so that he could answer any questions the customers had. The real key to his success, however, was that Marco's personality was simply infectious, he was one of those people very few could dislike.

He and Santiago were the only young people around. They took note of one another, but it took weeks for them to connect. Each time they encountered each other at the museum, either Santiago had a large tour group with him, or Marco was busy with a customer in the store.

When they had a chance to finally speak, they liked each other instantly. Santiago had been in San Miguel for a couple of years at this point, and had many acquaintances. He was never bored or lonely in his free time, yet had nobody he could honestly call a true friend. Meeting Marco was a turning point for Santiago. He began to feel like San Miguel de Allende was home. He missed Elena, but realized there was really no going back.

At the tour company, Santiago could only accept Spanish-speaking groups. It was the only thing holding him back from a modest, but comfortable, income. He decided to work on his English, knowing he would get much more work if he did.

There was a group of expat American benefactors who lived in San Miguel. They sponsored free English classes at the community center.

Santiago had nothing to lose. He wasn't working mornings at that moment. He walked to the building where the class was located. There was an open courtyard in the middle. The group was gathered there, preparing for class. Santiago took a seat at the table and looked around. Many of his classmates were older. Except one.

Daniel was born in Tamarindo, Costa Rica. Although the entire class was Spanish-speaking, the regional accents of the two made one another immediately identifiable as foreigners in Mexico. Daniel excitedly used expressions like *"pura vida"*. It amused Santiago to no end. Soon, the two were hanging out together outside of class.

According to Daniel, he had grown up essentially in paradise. He did have the look of someone who grew up near water; relaxed shoulders, an easy stride. His skin was dark from the sun, his hair always a little unkempt, like he didn't think much about it. He smiled often, but not to impress anyone.

Santiago was fascinated with the stories he told about the beautiful beaches in Costa Rica. Daniel's family was extremely poor. He had come to San Miguel de Allende for work, which he found as a taxi driver. Daniel loved to chat with the riders he picked up. That was the primary motivation behind his own desire to improve his English. San Miguel was full of American, Canadian and European tourists.

The two continued both their friendship and attending the free classes at the community center.

All the while, Santiago continued auditioning for role after role at the local theaters. Unbeknownst to him, it was that same Peruvian accent when he spoke Spanish, that was holding him back. Gradually, as a few years went by, he developed the ability to adopt a more localized version of his native tongue of Spanish. Suddenly, every once in a while, he would land a small role in a play.

CHAPTER SEVENTEEN

sun

With friends, he felt settled. There was happiness now, and pride in learning about his new culture. Santiago laughed uncontrollably along the rest of the English class when he was shown a picture of an avocado, and instinctively said "*palta*," the Peruvian word.

Daniel elbowed him, and Santiago burst out laughing as he corrected himself, "...*aguacate!*"

But he kicked him playfully as the two walked out, as he muttered *"pura vida"* sarcastically under his breath, just loud enough for Daniel to hear.

Santiago introduced Daniel to Marco. Both Marco and Daniel worked long hours. What little time was left, the three of them spent mostly together.

Santiago's schedule ebbed and flowed. The highs and lows of tourist season meant ever-changing hours at the tour company. If Santiago had a role in a play, rehearsals and performances would take up much of his time.

Usually, when he had time on his hands, he would continue the tradition Elena had taught him of volunteering at senior care facilities and reading to small children in schools.

None of the three had ideal living conditions. After closing night of Santiago's latest play, in his spare time, Santiago searched for an apartment they could share. Eventually, he found a walk-up in an older building in the Colonia San Rafael neighborhood. They moved in on the first of the following month, July 1, 1989.

The walls were faded ochre, dulled by time. The space lacked airiness, but if the windows were open, it was difficult to hear and impossible to sleep with the noise of the traffic from the street below.

They had very little.

Santiago managed, with permission, to take a few broken stage props. Forgotten remnants from plays that had closed years earlier, unused and long in the way, the theater manager was glad to see them go.

Daniel, easily the handiest of the three, repaired what he could. He also turned old backdrops into makeshift furniture.

A bookshelf made from a large piece of plywood painted with a garden scene. A table with half a sky. Each piece was a patchwork. Forests, cobbled streets, cityscapes… all cut mid-pattern, crafted into new shape.

"Good job, mate," Marco said, standing back to admire the result. "They look like a clown built them, but at least they're cheerful."

Daniel threw a yellow, papier-mâché sun at him. Marco ducked, laughing. The sun landed with a hollow thump in a corner, and there it stayed.

A rope ladder became a magazine rack. Their décor consisted of a wooden cutout palm tree, the sun, and a large stage pitchfork that no one wanted to claim.

Excess emerald green fabric from the costume department covered the windows. Years of watching set designers had left their mark on Santiago. He managed to artfully swag the fabric with the help of a staple gun so it hung just right. It caught the light in ways that made the space feel like something between a dressing room and a surreal, restless dream.

When Santiago handed his keys back to his former landlord, the man handed him a dusty cardboard box. Inside, he saw a few chipped plates, some cups and a few pieces of silverware.

"Some leftover items I don't need," the landlord said.

Santiago recognized with appreciation that the items weren't from the kitchen they had shared for three years. He suspected the older man had bought them secondhand, as a parting gift, but didn't want to admit it. He thanked the man. They shook hands, and Santiago carried the old box to the apartment, balancing it carefully so it wouldn't split apart as he walked.

There was a lot on Santiago's plate during the months that followed, but he didn't mind. The new apartment was incredible. At night, it had a view of the city's lights. He had never lived in a place with such a view before. To him, it was beautiful. The three roommates got along exceedingly well. Auditions were scheduled to begin the following week for the next performance, and Santiago believed he had an excellent chance of landing a role in the upcoming play.

Three days passed, then their first visitor arrived.

It was early evening. Santiago was lying on the floor of the living room, propped up on his elbows, reading a magazine, when a knock startled him.

An acquaintance from the theater stood in the doorway. That afternoon, a call had come in for Santiago. He would need to pay the long-distance charges, but he was welcome to use the theater's phone to call back the next day.

The caller was Antonio.

After a short battle with cancer, Elena had passed away.

CHAPTER EIGHTEEN

huaraz

Before Antonio finished his sentence, Santiago already knew there was only one reason why he would call him. Elena was the only mother he had ever known, and he had loved her with his whole heart. The call lasted less than two minutes. He could hear the animated voices of a play rehearsal going on in the next room. Until that moment, he hadn't realized how many parts of him were Elena. He felt like half his soul had left the earth with hers.

He was also confused. Antonio had offered to pay his rent for the month and cover a plane ticket so he could return to Peru for the funeral.

Santiago still carried bitterness toward Antonio, and part of him didn't want to accept. But his relationship with Elena won out. He did want to pay his respects, so he agreed. Antonio even arranged for a driver to take him to Mexico City, a journey of nearly four hours. From there, Santiago would return to his home country for the first time in almost four years.

After they arrived at Santiago's childhood home in Huaraz, Antonio's strange generosity faded. He returned to his usual, distant self. Santiago didn't care. He was there for Elena. He planned to pay his respects and leave as soon as he could.

The house was eerie without her.

Elena's funeral was well attended. Her community involvement ran deep, and the news of her early, untimely death aggrieved many.

Santiago barely noticed.

He found himself grieving more than Elena. Being back in Peru, he couldn't shake a strange disquiet. People here looked like him. They sounded like him. It felt distant and familiar all at once. It was home, but no longer his.

For the first time, he realized how much he loved San Miguel de Allende. But Peru, undeniably, still held something. A weight. A claim.

He understood now what it meant to have roots. Even if his own were unknown to him, he could feel them here.

Still, he knew this would likely be his last visit. With Elena gone, what reason would there be to return? The permanence of that was overwhelming.

The gathering after the service was a blur. Normally, he would have looked forward to the traditional Peruvian dishes being served there. The delicious smells of *Caldo de Gallina*, tamales, rice and potatoes filled the community hall, but Santiago had no appetite.

The fellowship continued around him. Beer and pisco flowed liberally. The gathering continued for hours.

Eventually, only he and Antonio remained in the hall. Antonio seemed drunk, but together they wiped down the metal tables and folded the chairs. They stacked them quietly and headed into the hallway, toward the front doors.

Suddenly, Antonio collapsed onto a wooden bench that lined the hall. At first, it looked to Santiago like a drunken stumble, but after a moment he realized that Antonio intended to sit. The way he looked up told Santiago he wanted him to sit down too.

Reluctantly, Santiago sat beside him.

Antonio buried his face in his hands and began to sob.

After a long pause, he spoke.

"Santiago," he said, catching his breath. "I am well aware of the feelings you carry toward me."

Santiago kept his eyes down.

"I am deserving of your contempt. I most surely am. I am even deserving of the very hatred of God. I did not deserve Elena. She did not deserve me. I married her knowing there was infertility in my family. And I knew she wanted children."

Santiago was still. He had expected nothing like this. Words of grief about Elena might have made sense. But this was something else entirely. Whatever it was, he wasn't in the mood.

Antonio fidgeted. He sat back and crossed his legs. His foot bounced. Santiago felt the bench shift beneath them each time his heel hit the floor. The hallway had gone dark. Light from the narrow windows near the doors reached across the floor.

Several times, Antonio opened his mouth to speak, but stopped.

He was unsteady. Whether from alcohol or nerves, Santiago could not tell.

When the words came, they arrived suddenly.

"Santiago, I have sinned. Elena never knew. It was my brother who impregnated Ana Lucia with you. I am deceitful. I am responsible for a rape. I brought him to her in secret to bear a child. It was Hermelinda's idea! She said it had been done before."

He took a breath.

"I did not want to do it. I only wanted to give Elena the child she so deeply desired. I knew my brother could father a child, while I could not."

Antonio was sweating now.

"After you were born, it became impossible to claim you. Sister Hermelinda planned on allowing me access, but then she died suddenly. Sister Pilar knew nothing about our arrangement."

Santiago had no idea who these people were. Antonio continued.

"I was willing to meet with Don Fernando as many times as needed to convince him to give you to Elena. And in the end, I did answer her prayers for a baby of her own. But guilt has consumed me ever since."

Something gave way inside Santiago.

Whatever was said next, Santiago never heard. He wanted to shut it all out. He distracted himself by thinking about the important audition he was missing. It was the only coping mechanism he could think of in that moment to try. Physically, he felt hot and sick. His skin burned. His stomach turned.

He wanted to be back in San Miguel. But apparently there was business to attend.

The next morning, Santiago and Antonio rode to the estate attorney's office. Antonio drove silently, his face as parched as the woven sweater of unbleached yarn he always wore over a button-down shirt. Sober now, he said nothing about the conversation they'd had the night before. Santiago sat in the passenger seat of Antonio's yellowish-brown 1978 Datsun 120Y. He leaned his head against the glass and looked out as they drove through the streets of Huaraz. He watched, and remembered.

The two were shown in. The office was a throwback to the mid-sixties in Peru. Wooden paneled walls and retro lighting that was not quite back in style yet, surrounded a desk with two visitor's chairs placed in front of it.

They were invited to sit. The chairs were a low, squarish design, with metal legs and green woolen upholstery that looked nubbed and pilled with wear.

Santiago watched Antonio's face as the attorney spoke at length about the "life estate", the combined assets Antonio and Elena had accumulated over the course of their marriage. Santiago knew Antonio's expressions too well. Was that an "as long as I'm alive, you won't see a penny" smirk he caught in his peripheral vision? Maybe. But Antonio would have been wrong.

Antonio looked ready to leave once the lawyer finished speaking about the joint estate. Then the attorney began to explain a second matter.

It concerned an inheritance from Elena's mother.

Elena had lost her mother nearly eighteen years before her own death. Antonio hadn't been able to accompany her to the funeral. Work, he said. She traveled alone to Yungay, attended the service, and visited her sister at the convent. It was during that visit that Sister Pilar told her about Ana Lucia's third pregnancy.

Elena received a modest inheritance from her mother. It came with a handwritten letter. Rosa María Teresa Fernández-Salazar had never learned to write, but with help, she had left her daughter a final wish.

August 15, 1964

My dearest daughter Elena,

I am including this letter among the papers for my last will and testament. Please do not grieve the loss of me. I have adored you as my child, and I have lived long.

You have, many times, come to me in sadness. I have understood for many years now that you wish for a baby, and no pregnancy comes.

It is a modest amount I am able to leave with you. I wish it were more. With it, I would like for you to see a doctor, a specialist. My hope is that you will be able to find out why you pray for a child who has not yet arrived. With these funds, I hope it is possible for you to be blessed with the miracle of a baby, my grandchild.

Con todo mi amor.

Your loving mother,

Rosa María Teresa Fernández-Salazar

Elena was not in the habit of keeping things from her husband. Initially, she struggled. This was her mother's dying wish. Would staying quiet be deception, or protection?

She knew Antonio couldn't bear the thought that it was likely himself incapable of conceiving a child. In a country where large families were the norm, his relatives were few, and many had no children at all. At family gatherings, she would sometimes overhear a cousin or aunt mention a family history of infertility, usually by accident. Antonio never noticed. Or pretended not to.

Elena herself couldn't bear the idea of searching for answers, if devastating her husband would be the outcome.

She didn't want to embarrass him. So, she told no one.

Instead, she stopped at the bank on her way back from Yungay. There, she placed most of the inheritance and her mother's letter in a safety deposit box. At home, she gave her husband a much smaller sum and explained that years of in-home nursing care had left little of her mother's finances behind. This, she told him, was all that remained.

Some of that was true, Elena reasoned.

Any guilt she felt dissolved when Antonio used a large portion of the shared funds to once again bail out his brother, who was always finding himself in one predicament or another. Elena had always viewed her husband's indulgence of her brother-in-law as enabling and counterproductive. He would never learn.

Though Elena would never use the money to visit a fertility doctor, even when finances were tight, she would not dishonor her mother's final wish. The money, and the letter, sat in the box, untouched.

It would be several years before Santiago came into her life. At some point, months or years after his arrival at their home, Elena remembered the long-forgotten money.

At once, she knew. The money would go to a child her mother would have adored. Because he was Ana Lucia's child, Santiago was their mother's biological grandchild.

Secretly, she updated her own will.

She knew her mother would have wholeheartedly approved.

CHAPTER NINETEEN

día de los muertos

Antonio pulled the car up to the airport's departures curb. Santiago grabbed his bag from the back seat. As he leaned in to close the passenger door, he simply asked, "Where is your brother now?"

"My brother died three years ago," Antonio replied, without emotion. "Cirrhosis of the liver."

Santiago shut the door and the car pulled away.

Back in San Miguel de Allende, Santiago had missed the audition. The money he received was not enough for him to be set for life, yet it was stabilizing. He opened the first account he'd ever had and deposited the funds.

As he left the bank, he felt a mix of gratitude and grief. He knew this would probably be the last tangible trace of Elena in this life.

The weeks that followed were dark. Tour season was slow. Posters and ads for the upcoming play, one he was not a part of, were all over town. Santiago hated leaving the apartment. He felt like a stranger, both in Peru and here. He still grieved Elena's death. He managed to work just enough so that he didn't need to dip into the money left to him by Elena, but he was barely getting by.

In town, festive preparations were well underway for the Day of the Dead festival. The highly anticipated celebrations had been among Santiago's favorites since childhood. A tradition he happily carried on with his friends in Mexico.

This year felt different. Santiago was in no mood.

In the apartment, Marco stood in the doorway to Santiago's room. He lay in bed, half propped up, slouching.

"You have been sulking for weeks, my friend," he teased.

Daniel walked up to stand beside them. Santiago's mouth twisted as he tried not to laugh at the sight of the two of them, who barely fit in the doorway. Both friends noticed.

"Come to the festival with us tonight!" demanded Marco with a wide smile.

Daniel whined dramatically, pretending to cry. "It won't be the same without you…"

The actor in Santiago could not fail to react with awe. In fact, he fully revered their brief, improvised performance for its sheer perfection. Two amateurs, who had inadvertently achieved what actors spend a career trying to develop. This was undeniably professional-level persuasiveness. This short exchange had been flawlessly executed. The pair, as a mismatched storm front. Playing off one another. Modeling an avatar of Santiago refusing to turn pity into spectacle, so that he could take note. Using levity to awaken something in his own brain. Their timing, breathtakingly on point. Irresistible.

Santiago went, but he didn't dress up, which was remarkably out of character for him.

The town's central plaza was packed. The atmosphere was full of laughter and music. Several mariachi bands were there, positioned close enough to the center of the crowd to draw attention, but far enough apart so they could be heard clearly. On a typical night, especially on the weekend, you might find a four- or five-piece ensemble. But tonight, they had come with extras. One band had fourteen musicians. There was even a harp.

Ten-foot-high puppet-like figures made of papier-mâché, cloth, and wood roamed the square, posing for pictures. Called *mojigangas*, they were elaborate costumes made to resemble various characters: skeletons, a bride and groom, witches. Santiago had worn one once, a cowboy. He must have posed for a thousand pictures that night.

He moved carefully around a *mojiganga* resembling a saint. Suddenly, he felt a cold, sticky liquid spill all over his body and clothes.

He looked up to meet the green eyes of a pale, white man about his height, maybe five or six years older. The man was standing in an impossibly tight crowd, holding an empty plastic cup, still dripping. He looked mortified, and mumbled something unintelligible in British-accented English that Santiago didn't catch.

Neither spoke. As an actor, the state of speechlessness was rare for Santiago.

After a few seconds, the man began to profusely apologize in a mix of English and excellent Spanish. The evening, the weeks prior—it had all been a lot for Santiago. It took him a moment to regain his usual charm.

The man continued to apologize, his Spanish smooth but British. He began to overshare.

"Hello, uh, I'm John, and as maybe you can tell, ehh, I'm British," he stammered. "But, you see, I do live here. I am most certainly NOT a tourist!" he added proudly, as if getting a drink spilled on you by a local was somehow better than by a tourist.

Santiago couldn't help but smile at the awkwardness. The *encantadorito* in him returned.

"Don't worry about it. No, seriously, it really is okay." He gave John a brilliant smile, hoping it would relax him. "I'm Santiago."

John exhaled three times in quick succession, then steadied himself. Whether it was courage or British manners, John himself would never be sure.

"Have you eaten?" he asked.

Are you kidding? Santiago thought. *With these prices?* He was still pretty broke. He simply shook his head.

"Well then," John said, more confident now, "as an apology, I simply must buy you dinner. Come on now, where do you live? Let's get you into some dry clothes, and then we'll go to a very nice restaurant. It's one of my personal favorites. I believe you'll like it very much. They have a wide variety of dishes to choose from."

Santiago looked at John. John blinked back, nervously.

In that moment, something passed between them. Something ancient.

Back in the present, Santiago knew a rejection would deprive John of his chance to make it right. And it looked like that chance mattered to him. Not wanting to disappoint, and also quite hungry, Santiago agreed.

Twenty minutes later, freshly washed and dressed, he walked to their meeting place by the clock tower. John was already there, waiting patiently. He smiled when he saw Santiago approaching.

They dined on a rooftop with lights and potted plants between cozy tables. An elegant restaurant like this was a first for Santiago. It looked like many of the patrons had just left closing night of the play. Noticing Santiago watching them closely, John asked if he had seen the play.

He continued to study John's features. His eyes were still a little nervous, but his face was compassionate, kind. Santiago had not the slightest idea what it meant to belong. But he knew how it felt when no one asked him to leave. He instinctively trusted John. So, he shared an abbreviated version of the story. Acting was his own profession. He had been in several performances at that theater before. He called Elena his mother when he spoke of her passing and the need to travel to Peru for the funeral.

Something in John shifted.

He expressed sympathy for the loss of Elena, of course. But then, he remembered where he had seen Santiago before.

"You know, Santiago, when I first saw you, I *knew* I recognized you from somewhere!" John said, suddenly intrigued. "Did you not play Leonardo in *Bodas de Sangre* a while back?"

A single sentence. An instant bond.

John had adored the performing arts since he was a boy. He never had aspirations to act, but never, ever missed a performance.

The moment fully realized. He was in awe of Santiago. And Santiago, of John.

Eventually, Santiago learned that John was five years older. He had impeccable manners, of course. Now calm, John was soft-spoken and articulate. They talked for hours.

"Thank you so much," Santiago said as they walked back through the cobbled streets, past the Parroquia de San Miguel Arcángel, toward the plaza.

"Ha!" John laughed. "It was the very least I could do after that debacle I caused."

Some distance behind them, the festival was still going on, but quieter now.

Then John paused.

"It's a pleasure to meet you, Santiago." Like a proper Brit, he extended his hand.

Santiago shook it, then felt compelled to hug him.

They parted at the plaza. Heading to their separate homes, neither doubted they had just met *the one*.

CHAPTER TWENTY

the photograph

In that moment, just after their two lives intersected, before anything had been said, everything already felt as if it were at risk.

Santiago hadn't intended to want anything. But something in the way John looked at him, with steadiness and unguarded warmth, made wanting unavoidable. It was too early to name what it was or to know if it would last. Still, Santiago already feared what it might mean to lose something he didn't even have.

Evening became morning, which turned quickly into weeks.

John and Santiago continued to share stories and imagine versions of what might come next. It deepened their bond, without either of them trying.

Santiago could make John laugh like no one else. They had fun.

Sometimes they took short vacations, something Santiago had never done before. They got along. They made space for each other's strangeness. What began as curiosity softened into care. Then, with time and no ceremony, into something real.

He felt welcome, and stayed at John's place most of the time. The apartment he shared with Daniel and Marco felt empty so often anyway. The two had been working long hours.

Before they met, John had a single bedside table. One evening, walking home after grabbing a bite to eat, they passed a small furniture store. John clasped Santiago's elbow and guided him into the store.

"Would you help me pick out a proper set of *two* bedside tables?" he asked.

It was the first new furniture Santiago had ever helped select. He had a strong, latent, talent for interior design that came alive in that moment. It was exciting. He helped John purchase two small nightstands they both really liked.

When Santiago first saw it, the apartment had been nicely furnished, but didn't look complete. It had "good bones", as they say. John's furniture selections were tasteful. The only thing missing was a bit of layering. Over the years, they shopped for the rest. Santiago's eye for décor made the apartment feel cozier, more like a home. It also elevated the space to the level of hosting guests.

Elena had taught Santiago to cook and garden. He prepared nightly meals for John. If Santiago was working, there would be a plate of food, carefully wrapped, waiting for John when he got home. They didn't have a terrace, but for the first time, there were houseplants indoors.

Seven years later, Santiago stirred within the high thread count sheets in John's bed. Even after all the years, he still maintained his apartment with Marco and Daniel. John fully expected Santiago to move in to his upscale flat at some point. He mentioned it from time to time. Santiago loved John with all of his heart. Still, even then, it was all so surreal.

These were thoughts of impostor syndrome that Santiago buried deeply, or at least he tried. They cropped up more often than he cared to admit. Yes, he absolutely adored John. Could a Peruvian orphan be with someone like John? In a country that was foreign to both, no less. He guessed he would never truly trust the pervasive sense he had that they belonged together.

It was then that he realized he didn't know who he was.

The morning light was coming through the colonial style windows. John was typically an early riser, so it was no surprise that he was already out of bed. Santiago's phone vibrated on the nightstand beside him, clacking on the thin layer of glass John had placed there to protect the wood tops. The noise startled and distracted him.

He managed a weary "Hello." The caller spoke. He listened.

At the office, John had wrapped up a morning meeting with clients. He glanced at his watch. 10:10. Morning tea time for John was always around 10:00. He walked to the closest café, where he ordered an Earl Gray every weekday morning around the same time.

When John arrived, much to his absolute shock, Santiago was already seated at one of John's usual tables, waiting for him.

"I knew you'd be taking a break around now" Santiago explained in a low voice, almost a whisper, looking around the café, trying not to make a scene. "I hope it's okay I join you."

John nodded. Santiago looked up. Instantly, his eyes brightened, and he said with a giant smile, in a loud, enthusiastic tone, completely different from the one he had used before, "I got the part!"

This was his big break. They had been nervously waiting since the audition. John, at times, was more of a wreck than Santiago. He could tell John was trying to act calm, but his hands gave him away every time they talked about the audition, which John seemed to be mentioning all the time. It made him smile. He hadn't felt that kind of quiet care since Elena.

It was Santiago's first lead role at Ángela Peralta Theater, San Miguel's largest. He would play the lead role of *Don Juan Tenorio* in the play of the same name.

The two hugged in utter excitement. John's hand shook as he tried to drink his cup of tea. His concentration at the office would be completely shot for the rest of the day after hearing this news.

The next day, the afternoon rain subsided long enough for the two of them to accomplish their goal. John had again been working long hours. It wasn't often they had time to venture out during daylight.

"Alright then, smile!" said John brightly as he took a photo. Behind Santiago was a large sign advertising the play, with his name on it in prominent letters. The shutter clicked.

John proudly turned his phone to face Santiago, to show him the picture.

Santiago stared at the screen. He saw his own face beside the poster with his name in bold lettering. John had framed the shot carefully, like he was taking a portrait, not a picture.

He hardly recognized himself.

In the few days that followed, John knew he would need to move quickly. Rehearsals would begin next week. Santiago would have no time, nor much mental space for anything else but this phenomenal role, this incredible opportunity.

He texted Marco and Daniel. The three of them contacted any theater friends they knew of, who also agreed to spread the word. Although it had been some time since they had taken the English language class together, Daniel got in touch with the few friends they made there. Preparations for the celebratory party began.

The party was a huge success. John had splurged for the occasion. He reserved the entire shared rooftop patio of their apartment complex for the evening. It had a spectacular view of San Miguel de Allende from all sides.

Santiago's theater friends took care of the decorations with the flair you'd expect from a group of actors and stagehands. They designed black table centerpieces with clay comedy and tragedy masks, punctuated by tall yellow flowers. Strings of silver candle lanterns borrowed from the theater's prop room were hung overhead.

Marco and Daniel handled the setup. They climbed ladders, arranged chairs, and draped black and silver tablecloths to match the lanterns and centerpieces. They picked up mylar balloons with theater themes, mixed with plain black, yellow, and silver.

Drinks and appetizers flowed. Servers moved through the crowd with silver trays, offering miniature jicama tacos, chilled shrimp, mole-covered croquettes, ceviche spoons, and queso fundido tartlets.

At what seemed like just the right moment, the music quieted down, and the DJ handed John the microphone. Everyone cheered as he congratulated Santiago on his upcoming lead role in this important play.

News of this performance of the classic play, *Don Juan Tenorio*, was spreading quickly, far and wide. Theater management believed that Santiago was perfect for the role, and that the other cast members would also be excellent. Extra budget was allocated for set and costume design. Promotion of this performance would exceed anything they had done in the past.

John motioned for Santiago to join him alongside the DJ booth, where he still held the microphone. When Santiago reached him, everything grew quiet. A plan was set in motion.

He knelt down on one knee and asked Santiago to marry him.

The last time Santiago had felt this many emotions at once was in that dark hallway after Elena's celebration of life. That night, still in fresh, hot grief from the loss of Elena, Antonio had revealed his deepest secret. This moment had some of that confusion, and some of the same weight.

This was altogether different, yet the same. He felt the pain of feeling undeserving of John's deep love for him, juxtaposed with the warmth of his friends' genuine support, and of course his own undying devotion to John.

So many emotions present, seemingly simultaneously. All Santiago could do was weep quietly. John embraced him. The guests assumed, by John's reaction, that Santiago had accepted the proposal, but had spoken too quietly for them to hear. The party continued, even more festive than before. Santiago spent the rest of the evening never far from John, making sure they stayed connected. They both smiled and laughed together with the guests until the early morning hours when the last had finally gone home.

They said little. But when the lights went out, they hugged tight, and neither one let go.

CHAPTER TWENTY-ONE

cast

Santiago felt tired Sunday morning, but at least not too hungover. Still in bed, his thoughts raced. He wasn't stupid enough to let his past stand in the way of what he knew was a once-in-a-lifetime love, one he could feel was real. John knew when to give him space, and did so. Even if it tortured him inside, he waited. Patiently. The proposal, rehearsals, opening night. Santiago had a lot on his mind, he reasoned.

Santiago's mind spun the same way each morning. And every time, he caught himself imagining what Antonio might have thought. He hated the intrusive thoughts. Sometimes, he imagined what it would have been like to grow up in San Miguel instead of Huaraz.

He had watched others fall into the same spirals. His theater manager, exceptionally talented, had refused better jobs at larger, more renowned theaters, out of fear. His first landlord, a caring, intelligent man, living too simple a life. Alone

Santiago recognized only he could stop his own spiral.

"Things will be good," he said out loud, to no one.

"I should marry John."

The following week, at Ángela Peralta Theater, John fiddled with the cuffs of Santiago's ruffled shirt.

"Don't lose these, 'ya handsome stud. They were my grandfather's," he said, concentrating. He fastened a pair of sterling silver and onyx cufflinks in a vintage, squared-off style at his wrist.

Over it, Santiago put on a long, velvet coat. It was blue with gold embroidery. He turned up his collar, checked his wig and walked on stage. Once seated at a barstool on a set resembling a tavern, he gave a nod to the stage crew, indicating it was time for the curtain to rise.

"¡Por donde se va al infierno!"

Santiago expertly stepped into the defiance and recklessness of a man nothing like himself. That first line, *whichever way leads to hell,* was a critical one. A dramatic entrance for the role. It was sink or swim. *Nothing like jumping right in,* Santiago had been thinking for months.

He heard claps as some of the audience reacted to the line. Santiago was satisfied. The delivery was as good as his best in rehearsals, maybe better.

Seated in the first row was the mayor of San Miguel de Allende and his wife. Next to her sat the wife of the mayor of Mexico City, and the woman's sister. Alongside them, a few local government officials, sponsors, patrons, two local journalists, and four people Santiago didn't recognize. John was in the second row.

Santiago gave a natural, organic performance. It was as if he became the character.

After the final bow, the atmosphere backstage was absolutely celebratory. The director had already popped the imported prosecco, and was drinking in delirious happiness and relief. Flowers were everywhere, turning the tired backstage space into something else entirely. It seemed like everyone in the acting profession in all of San Miguel had used their connections to be backstage tonight. Soon, the area was completely full of bodies. A line began to back up into the hallway as guests who had been seated in the auditorium were using the forward doors to exit the theater. It was difficult to move at all.

Seeing that the door would not close due to the crowd size, John made his way toward it. With some difficulty, dodging people left and right, he finally reached it. He began to greet people standing outside in his most diplomatic, British way. Someone had to explain there was no room, and that they would not be let in due to lack of space. In short, he was trying to do some crowd control. The people he spoke to were clearly disappointed to miss the chance to slip backstage and join the celebration. But John was so gracious that they couldn't be too angry at being turned away. He thanked each one for being there.

A group of actors left the room noisily, passing John on their way out. A sharply dressed man, on the younger side, took the opportunity to move into the newly-created empty space. He stepped up to John and shook his hand. John felt like he had seen this man somewhere before. He introduced himself only as Enrique. Hearing his voice and studying him a bit more, John now doubted he knew Enrique, but he instantly liked him just the same.

"This is my wife, Clara." Enrique continued. Clara was a plump woman in a floral dress with an innocent, kind face. She smiled sweetly at John by way of introduction, but didn't speak.

"My sister Luz…" Luz was taller than her sister-in-law, with more angled features. She had brown eyes and curly, dark hair.

"… and her husband, Eugenio," Enrique concluded. To John, Eugenio looked a bit nerdy. He looked at the floor, while his wife huffed about not being allowed to enter.

"Let's go," Luz demanded. "I told you this would be a waste of time." She took her husband's hand as a gesture to leave, but nobody moved.

Just then, Marco and Daniel moved past them, slapping one another on the back and poking fun at each other in the mock-brutal way close friends often do.

"Motherfucker!" laughed Daniel. Behind them, Santiago followed his two friends to the door to see them off. "Bye, you two id-" Santiago stopped as his eyes met John's. He was standing with the four people from the front row that Santiago had seen, but didn't recognize. Instinctively, Santiago knew it would be only a particularly special kind of guest who would be able to secure coveted front row seats on an opening night.

Before he had a chance to speak, Enrique stepped forward. Santiago looked up with him, curiosity in his bright, hazel eyes.

Enrique looked a few years older than him. He was dressed in black pants and a black dress shirt, with the collar unbuttoned. Underneath, a thick, gold Italian rope chain was barely visible around his neck.

"Good to meet you. I'll get right to the point; I don't want to interrupt the party," Enrique began. There was a slight accent there, barely noticeable. To Santiago, it sounded Peruvian. Yet, when he had first arrived in Mexico, his own dialect carried more of an Andean regional accent than this man's.

Santiago's thoughts were interrupted as Enrique continued. "I've been doing quite a bit of research since I first saw an ad on social media for this play several weeks ago. Please tell me, are you from Peru?"

Luz visibly scoffed. Santiago answered that, yes, he was Peruvian. Born in Yungay, grew up in Huaraz, he told Enrique.

Upon hearing Santiago's answer, something in Enrique's countenance shifted. A thousand synapses firing all at once. He paused. It appeared he was weighing carefully what he would ask next.

"I know this is an extremely odd question. I hope it is one you don't find too intrusive. Santiago, do you happen to have scars on your left forearm?"

At this point, Luz sighed loudly and turned to leave. Everyone else was captivated. Nothing so loud as that backstage area ever seemed so quiet. Santiago never understood what people meant when they said their "blood ran cold". In this moment, he knew.

John instinctively helped remove his grandfather's cufflink and rolled up Santiago's sleeve to reveal the scars. Enrique, Clara and Eugenio stared at them in awe.

Santiago looked up, and met Enrique's eyes. They were hazel. Identical in every way to his own.

"Let's go." Luz snapped.

Without looking up, now holding Santiago's forearm, examining it incredulously, Enrique answered his sister. He spoke softly.

"Don't walk out of here. Don't be a fool. This is our brother."

Two men who shared a mother. They stared at each other silently, in disbelief and wonder.

CHAPTER TWENTY-TWO

avalanche

The ranch of Don Fernando Javier Alarcón had been tragically buried under the avalanche following the Ancash earthquake. There were many casualties, including the Don himself, and the entire house of servants. Had he stayed, Santiago would have been among them.

It was not uncommon for Doña García to be out of the house for various reasons. She was something of a socialite in Yungay during that era. Normally, she left the children with the nanny, or Ama. A sixth sense told her to take them with her that day.

They had a few shops to visit when the earthquake struck. The lights in the store started to swing and flash. A few buzzed and appeared to short out. The customers were evacuated from the store, cutting their visit short.

Rumi wouldn't be arriving with the car for another half hour. It was cold, but the children were dressed warmly. Scared, but still resourceful, the Doña took the children by the hand and made her way to the park at the top of the hill, adjacent to the cemetery. The two children, feeling free after being indoors for months of winter, ran happily in the open space. She had been gazing at the ruffled, peach-colored flowers in her shopping basket. She looked up and watched in horror as the avalanche destroyed the town before her eyes.

The three of them had fallen upon hard times for quite a while. They were left devastated. It would take eighteen months for insurance to finally pay out. Once it finally did, they relocated. Nuevo Yungay was the town that was rebuilt nearby, strategically placed in a safer location.

A large ranch would have been far too much for a widow to manage. Doña García moved herself and her two children into a modest but well-appointed home. Nuevo Yungay was beautiful, if sorrowful. The mountains were more distant now, still the same majestic backdrop, but no longer a threat. The town sat high on a hill, eerily quiet, with clouds and wind moving through it as if it weren't there. No one who lived there had survived without the trauma of the quake.

Yungay had been old, and parts of it had been crumbling. The newness was clean, almost cleansing. At the same time, it was a constant reminder of what had been lost. Historyless. Generic.

Even so, it was a safe and peaceful place for Enrique and Luz to grow up.

Whenever the two asked about their father, their mother would answer politely and sufficiently. On her own, Doña García didn't often speak of her late husband. She did, however, remember one person fondly: her beautiful former assistant, Isabel Cristina. That one had been her favorite.

It was not until she was on her deathbed a year or so prior to that night that she finally opened up to her children about their origins. She told them she was not their biological mother.

Enrique admitted that he would never have known about Santiago's existence if it weren't for his sister. He wouldn't have pressed, although he did want to know more.

Luz felt betrayed, lied to. Even though her mother was frail, she wasn't afraid to press for an explanation.

Surprisingly, Doña García didn't seem all that reluctant to comply. Both brother and sister suspected that the truth had been weighing heavily on her. At that point, she tired easily, so the story unfolded over several visits.

At first, they heard pretty much what they expected to. Their parents couldn't have children, so they adopted.

But as Doña García continued, the story grew more mysterious.

From what they could gather, on several occasions, their mother had seen their father meet with the older nun, Sister Hermelinda. That was where her suspicions began.

One Sunday, before they left for church, she saw him put a large roll of bills in his pocket. She watched as they passed the collection plate. He reached into a different pocket, and put a much smaller amount of money in it, just a few coins.

When they came home, he casually draped his pants over a chair in the bedroom. She checked his pockets. The cash wasn't there.

In her hospital bed, Doña García lowered her chin and closed her eyes. She didn't say any more.

A few days passed before the subject was raised again. Surprisingly, this time the Doña lifted her index finger, raised an eyebrow, and said, "That's right, I did have something I wanted to tell you about that."

She shifted slightly, her fingers brushing the edge of the blanket.

"I remember the words… Bless me, Father, for I have sinned. And the two of you," she said, looking at them, "I hope that you can forgive me."

Her gaze wandered to a corner of the room, unfocused.

"I didn't even know what kind of sin it was. Suspicion? Cowardice? I had to say something. I had to say it out loud."

A pause. Then faster, as though the memory were overtaking her. She sounded more like herself now.

"I told him, Father Rafael, that your father once said he had arranged something wonderful. A blessing. That he'd found children. That a nun at the convent helped him. He said the mother couldn't keep you. That it was all handled. Discreet. Clean. He made it sound like a kindness."

Her voice wavered.

"I told myself it was a gift from God. That we were stepping in. Maybe we'd saved someone shame, or rescued a child without parents."

She blinked quickly.

"I told Father Rafael what I had seen. I told him about that day before mass that he gave money to Sister Hermelinda. My children, she slipped it into her sleeve like it was nothing. Cold woman, that Hermelinda. No warmth in her eyes."

Her eyes filled with tears. She looked tired now.

"I knew I shouldn't doubt my husband. The two of you were a blessing, clearly brought to me by God, so why was I questioning this miracle in my own life?"

She looked at them.

"I never met your mother. Not once. I never saw her face. There was no blessing. No priest. Just your father bringing you into the house one day, wrapped in blankets, beautiful. Perfect in every way."

Her breathing turned shallow. Her words came slower, but heavier. They asked if she wanted to finish the story next time. She didn't seem to hear, and went on.

"I told the Father that I was grateful. Still am. But that doesn't make it right."

Silence. Then, faintly:

"I heard him breathe. It's hard to explain. I know it sounds strange. A sound caught in his throat. That was the first moment I knew. He knew something."

A long silence passed. They thought she might be finished. Then, "I asked if you were taken. If they'd been taken."

Her fingers twitched against the sheets.

"I wasn't supposed to know that. So, you understand, I did sin, honestly. I stood behind the door when Sister Pilar spoke to him. I listened."

Doña García had overheard Sister Pilar say that Ana Lucia was disabled. She distinctly heard the nun remind her husband that the poor woman had been sexually assaulted.

It all made sense.

There was nothing to do. No redemption. The woman couldn't care for her children, so life went on. She loved and raised her children.

Then, Isabel Cristina arrived with Santiago at the ranch. Enrique looked at Santiago, whose eyes told him was trying hard to focus, to process it all. "Yes, you were there!" he said.

Knowing Isabel Cristina had come from the convent, Doña García became curious about the origins of this third child. Their family was already complete, and Sister Hermelinda had passed away. Who was *this* child?

His sister could remember a time when her parents were warm with one another. A time when her father looked at her mother with genuine love, and she returned his affection. Enrique only remembered them being distant with one another. This, Enrique explained, was probably the point where their mother began to distrust their father.

They asked her if she ever told their father that she knew. Their mother nodded bravely from the bed.

"Yes, I did. I told him I knew, and he didn't deny it. I asked him if the third child was also his, and he said no."

She told them she believed that Don Fernando was their biological father. Don Fernando had been a liar about many things. She had witnessed many of these lies firsthand. Instinctively, the Doña knew her husband was being truthful when he said he was not Santiago's father.

Still, she didn't intend to allow Santiago to grow up as an indentured servant, but she had time, she had thought. For the moment, the baby was being well cared for by Ama and Isabel Cristina. She would come up with a plan when the time was right.

Then there was the murder.

Enrique explained that his mother never spoke to them of the tragic accident involving Isabel Cristina. She didn't have to. The whole town knew. He told Santiago that Luz found out through the grapevine about the scars on his arm from that fateful night his arm was injured as he fell from Isabel Cristina's arms when Don Fernando fired his gun at her.

As he spoke his sister's name, Enrique involuntarily cringed. Luz looked at him. He immediately wished he could take it back. She was triggered. It was time to go.

CHAPTER TWENTY-THREE

standing still

Nothing extraordinary happened in the months that followed. And that was the change. Santiago woke, breathed, and did not long for anywhere else. The voices didn't leave him, but they were mere spectators now, a group of cantankerous commentators from the mezzanine.

It became easier for Santiago to let go of Antonio, or maybe for the anger he felt toward Antonio to let go of him. Santiago no longer felt he had to hold on to an uncle he never asked for, that impostor he had for a father all those years. For so long, he had clung to what he believed were the last threads of family.

Now, something unexpected had begun to take root. The bond with Enrique filled a space in him he hadn't realized was empty.

Enrique stayed in touch, always, but never out of obligation.

In his new state of mind, the absolute first order of business for Santiago was to accept John's proposal.

As often happens, when we change, life around us begins to change as well. Wedding planning was in full swing. Clara announced her first pregnancy. Santiago was going to be an uncle.

After hearing the news, it seemed like there wasn't a stuffed animal or onesie in all of San Miguel de Allende that "Uncle John" could resist buying. Enrique and Clara were deeply touched by John's gentle enthusiasm.

Santiago, John, Enrique and Clara would remain close for life.

One quiet Saturday, bored at home, Enrique FaceTimed Santiago. They talked for over an hour. Mostly laughter. Mostly joy. Brotherly bonding. At one point, Enrique brought up the subject of their sister, Luz.

She still had not become comfortable with her newfound half-brother.

Enrique hoped Santiago could forgive her.

It was a tragic loss that had driven him to seek out Santiago. After the death of the only mother they had ever known, Enrique and Luz had no surviving relatives. Clara had helped Enrique search. Eventually, they found Antonio. He told them Santiago had moved to San Miguel de Allende.

Then came the ad for *Don Juan Tenorio*. It had felt surreal.

Could this be the same Santiago?

They booked the trip, agreeing to see the play. If it wasn't him, they'd keep looking.

"Imagine losing every relative, school friend, teacher. Every familiar face at the corner store, in church, the bus driver," Enrique said.

Santiago couldn't begin to understand that pain.

"It's the same pain," Enrique added gently. "The pain that made me find you is the same pain that causes Luz to shut down. I think it triggers something in her when she sees you. Please don't be angry that she rejects you."

Santiago looked at his brother through his screen with understanding eyes. They both instinctively knew he got the message.

After a pause, to lighten the heavy mood, Santiago burst out laughing with a scoff, and, as actors are prone to do, suddenly crafted a brand new act, in a louder voice:

"I grew up gay in Peru. Then I became an actor... I can *take* rejection!" He smiled mischievously, and both of them laughed before saying goodbye.

The wedding of Santiago and John was truly beautiful.

Enrique and Clara made a second trip from Peru just six months later to attend. Clara fought morning sickness to be there.

about the author

Harrison Rose Tate is an accomplished nonfiction writer, chronicler, and archivist whose work, spanning essays, articles, professional and technical publications, has reached wide audiences for over two decades, often without a byline.

She has lived and traveled extensively throughout the world.

The Tour Guide is her debut novella, written after a chance encounter in San Miguel de Allende. Though she never planned to become a novelist, this was a story which needed to be told.

acknowledgments

An empty café. Me, not particularly present. Him, relaxed, maybe a bit bored, then animated. He spoke quickly but softly, naturally but with the definite traces of an actor's presence.

A time and a place. Just words. No notes. No intention to do anything but have a conversation. He didn't speak English, and my Spanish is okay at best. Soon, I was captivated, but only on a personal level.

The tour guide himself is the true author here. I am grateful that I seemed approachable enough for him to trust me with this story. I didn't immediately decide to write it.

Though a few names have been changed and details adapted, the emotional truth of what happened is honored here. In this context, given the tragic Ancash earthquake of 1970, that statement carries weight. I was both told this story and wrote this story in memory of those who lived in Ancash in the year 1970, those who survived and those who didn't.

I also thank John, whom I did get to meet, and all in San Miguel de Allende and in the communities of Peru whose presence and insight allowed this story to endure. Thanks, too, to beautiful Lake Elsinore, California, for being the most stunning, inspirational backdrop, as my fingers tapped the keys.

Finally, gratitude to those close to me who vocally encouraged me to share this work, even though fiction was never the plan. And to you, the reader, for holding space for what might otherwise have been forgotten.

thank you

If you enjoyed The Tour Guide, please consider leaving a review or sharing it with others.

Independent authors don't have large publishing houses to back them or to promote their work. If this story reaches new readers, it will be solely because someone like you felt it was worth passing on.

THE TOUR GUIDE

THE TOUR GUIDE